The Prairie

Arthur Stringer

Alpha Editions

This edition published in 2024

ISBN 9789361474644

Design and Setting By

Alpha Editions

www.alphaedis.com

Email - info@alphaedis.com

As per information held with us this book is in Public Domain.
This book is a reproduction of an important historical work.
Alpha Editions uses the best technology to reproduce historical work
in the same manner it was first published to preserve its original nature.
Any marks or number seen are left intentionally to preserve.

Contents

Thursday the Nineteenth	- 1 -
Saturday the Twenty-first	- 7 -
Monday the Twenty-third	- 13 -
Wednesday the Twenty-fifth	- 16 -
Thursday the Twenty-sixth	- 19 -
Saturday the Twenty-eighth	- 22 -
Wednesday the First	- 24 -
Thursday the Second	- 26 -
Friday the Third	- 28 -
Saturday the Fourth	- 29 -
Monday the Sixth	- 31 -
Wednesday the Eighth	- 34 -
Saturday the Tenth	- 37 -
Sunday the Eleventh	- 39 -
Monday the Twelfth	- 40 -
Sunday the Eighteenth	- 43 -
Monday the Nineteenth	- 44 -
Tuesday the Twentieth	- 45 -
Thursday the Twenty-second	- 49 -
Saturday the Twenty-fourth	- 51 -
Tuesday the Twenty-seventh	- 54 -
Thursday the Twenty-ninth	- 56 -
Friday the Fifth	- 58 -
Sunday the Seventh	- 59 -
Tuesday the Ninth	- 60 -

Saturday the Twenty-first	- 62 -
Sunday the Twenty-ninth	- 65 -
Monday the Seventh	- 66 -
Friday the Eleventh	- 67 -
Sunday the Thirteenth	- 68 -
Wednesday the Sixteenth	- 69 -
Sunday the Twentieth	- 70 -
Sunday the Twenty-seventh	- 71 -
Wednesday the Thirtieth	- 72 -
Thursday the Thirty-first	- 73 -
Sunday the Third	- 76 -
Thursday the Seventh	- 78 -
Saturday the Ninth	- 79 -
Monday the Eleventh	- 80 -
Tuesday the Nineteenth	- 83 -
Sunday the Thirty-first	- 85 -
Tuesday the Ninth	- 86 -
Wednesday the Seventeenth	- 87 -
Thursday the Twenty-fifth	- 88 -
Tuesday the Second	- 89 -
Thursday the Fourth	- 90 -
Wednesday the Seventeenth	- 91 -
Saturday the Twenty-seventh	- 92 -
Tuesday the Sixth	- 93 -
Monday the Twelfth	- 94 -
Tuesday the Twentieth	- 95 -
Monday the Twenty-sixth	- 96 -

Wednesday the Twenty-eighth	- 97 -
Monday the Second	- 98 -
Thursday the Fifth	- 99 -
Tuesday the Tenth	- 101 -
Monday the Sixteenth	- 103 -
Tuesday the Twenty-fourth	- 104 -
Friday the Third	- 105 -
Thursday the Ninth	- 106 -
Wednesday the Fifteenth	- 108 -
Friday the Seventeenth	- 109 -
Saturday the Nineteenth	- 110 -
Friday the Twenty-eighth	- 111 -
Saturday the Twenty-ninth	- 112 -
Sunday the Thirtieth	- 113 -
Tuesday the First	- 114 -
Monday the Seventh	- 117 -
Sunday the Thirteenth	- 119 -
Monday the Twenty-eighth	- 120 -
Saturday the Second	- 121 -
Wednesday the Sixth	- 122 -
Tuesday the Twelfth	- 123 -
Thursday the Fourteenth	- 124 -
Wednesday the Fifth	- 125 -
Sunday the Ninth	- 127 -
Monday the Tenth	- 128 -
Tuesday the Eleventh	- 129 -
Wednesday the Thirteenth	- 130 -

Thursday the Fourteenth	- 131 -
Friday the Fifteenth	- 132 -
Saturday the Sixteenth	- 133 -
Monday the Seventeenth	- 135 -
Wednesday the Nineteenth	- 136 -
Friday the Twenty-first	- 137 -
Monday the Twelfth	- 142 -
Wednesday the Fourteenth	- 143 -
Thursday the Fifteenth	- 145 -
Friday the Sixteenth	- 147 -
Sunday the Eighteenth	- 150 -
Sunday the Twenty-fifth	- 151 -
Tuesday the Twenty-seventh	- 152 -
Wednesday the Twenty-eighth	- 153 -
Friday the Thirtieth	- 154 -
Sunday the First	- 155 -

Thursday the Nineteenth

Splash!... That's me, Matilda Anne! That's me falling plump into the pool of matrimony before I've had time to fall in love! And oh, Matilda Anne, Matilda Anne, I've *got* to talk to you! You may be six thousand miles away, but still you've got to be my safety-valve. I'd blow up and explode if I didn't express myself to some one. For it's so lonesome out here I could go and commune with the gophers. This isn't a twenty-part letter, my dear, and it isn't a diary. It's the coral ring I'm cutting my teeth of desolation on. For, every so long, I've simply got to sit down and talk to some one, or I'd go mad, clean, stark, staring mad, and bite the tops off the sweet-grass! It may even happen this will never be sent to you. But I like to think of you reading it, some day, page by page, when I'm fat and forty, or, what's more likely, when Duncan has me chained to a corral-post or finally shut up in a padded cell. For you were the one who was closest to me in the old days, Matilda Anne, and when I was in trouble you were always the staff on which I leaned, the calm-eyed Tillie-on-the-spot who never seemed to fail me! And I think you will understand.

But there's so much to talk about I scarcely know where to begin. The funny part of it all is, I've gone and married the *Other Man*. And you won't understand that a bit, unless I start at the beginning. But when I look back, there doesn't seem to be any beginning, for it's only in books that things really begin and end in a single lifetime.

Howsomever, as Chinkie used to say, when I left you and Scheming Jack in that funny little stone house of yours in Corfu, and got to Palermo, I found Lady Agatha and Chinkie there at the Hotel des Palmes and the yacht being coaled from a tramp steamer's bunkers in the harbor. So I went on with them to Monte Carlo. We had a terrible trip all the way up to the Riviera, and I was terribly sea-sick, and those lady novelists who love to get their heroines off on a private yacht never dream that in anything but duckpond weather the ordinary yacht at sea is about the meanest habitation between Heaven and earth. But it was at Monte Carlo I got the cable from Uncle Carlton telling me the Chilean revolution had wiped out our nitrate mine concessions and that your poor Tabby's last little nest-egg had been smashed. In other words, I woke up and found myself a beggar, and for a few hours I even thought I'd have to travel home on that Monte Carlo Viaticum fund which so discreetly ships away the stranded adventurer before he musses up the Mediterranean scenery by shooting himself. Then I remembered my letter of credit, and firmly but sorrowfully paid off poor

Hortense, who through her tears proclaimed that she'd go with me anywhere, and without any thought of wages (imagine being hooked up by a maid to whom you were under such democratizing obligations!) But I was firm, for I knew the situation, might just as well be faced first as last.

So I counted up my letter of credit and found I had exactly six hundred and seventy-one dollars, American money, between me and beggary. Then I sent a cable to Theobald Gustav (so condensed that he thought it was code) and later on found that he'd been sending flowers and chocolates all the while to the Hotel de L'Athénée, the long boxes duly piled up in tiers, like coffins at the morgue. Then Theobald's aunt, the baroness, called on me, in state. She came in that funny, old-fashioned, shallow landau of hers, where she looked for all the world like an oyster-on-the-half-shell, and spoke so pointedly of the danger of international marriages that I felt sure she was trying to shoo me away from my handsome and kingly Theobald Gustav—which made me quite calmly and solemnly tell her that I intended to take Theobald out of under-secretaryships, which really belonged to Oppenheim romances, and put him in the shoe business in some nice New England town!

From Monte Carlo I scooted right up to Paris. Two days later, as I intended to write you but didn't, I caught the boat-train for Cherbourg. And there at the rail as I stepped on the *Baltic* was the Other Man, to wit, Duncan Argyll McKail, in a most awful-looking yellow plaid English mackintosh. His face went a little blank as he clapped eyes on me, for he'd dropped up to Banff last October when Chinkie and Lady Agatha and I were there for a week. He'd been very nice, that week at Banff, and I liked him a lot. But when Chinkie saw him "going it a bit too strong," as he put it, and quietly tipped Duncan Argyll off as to Theobald Gustav, the aforesaid D. A. bolted back to his ranch without as much as saying good-by to me. For Duncan Argyll McKail isn't an Irishman, as you might in time gather from that name of his. He's a Scotch-Canadian, and he's nothing but a broken-down civil engineer who's taken up farming in the Northwest. But I could see right away that he was a gentleman (I *hate* that word, but where'll you get another one to take its place?) and had known nice people, even before I found out he'd taught the Duchess of S. to shoot big-horn. He'd run over to England to finance a cooperative wheat-growing scheme, but had failed, because everything is so unsettled in England just now.

But you're a woman, and before I go any further you'll want to know what Duncan looks like.

Well, he's not a bit like his name. The West has shaken a good deal of the Covenanter out of him. He's tall and gaunt and wide-shouldered, and has brown eyes with hazel specks in them, and a mouth exactly like Holbein's

"Astronomer's," and a skin that is almost as disgracefully brown as an Indian's. On the whole, if a Lina Cavalieri had happened to marry a Lord Kitchener, and had happened to have a thirty-year-old son, I feel quite sure he'd have been the dead spit, as the Irish say, of my own Duncan Argyll. And Duncan Argyll, *alias* Dinky-Dunk, is rather reserved and quiet and, I'm afraid, rather masterful, but not as Theobald Gustav might have been, for with all his force the modern German, it seems to me, is like the bagpipes in being somewhat lacking in suavity.

And all the way over Dinky-Dunk was so nice that he almost took my breath away. He was also rather audacious, gritting his teeth in the face of the German peril, and I got to like him so much I secretly decided we'd always be good friends, old-fashioned, above-board, Platonic good friends. But the trouble with Platonic love is that it's always turning out too nice to be Platonic, or too Platonic to be nice. So I had to look straight at the bosom of that awful yellow-plaid English mackintosh and tell Dinky-Dunk the truth. And Dinky-Dunk listened, with his astronomer mouth set rather grim, and otherwise not in the least put out. His sense of confidence worried me. It was like the quietness of the man who is holding back his trump. And it wasn't until the impossible little wife of an impossible big lumberman from Saginaw, Michigan, showed me the Paris *Herald* with the cable in it about that spidery Russian stage-dancer, L———, getting so nearly killed in Theobald's car down at Long Beach, that I realized there *was* a trump card and that Dinky-Dunk had been too manly to play it.

I had a lot of thinking to do, the next three days.

When Theobald came on from Washington and met the steamer my conscience troubled me and I should still have been kindness itself to him, if it hadn't been for his proprietary manner (which, by the way, had never annoyed me before), coupled with what I already knew. We had luncheon in the Della Robbia room at the Vanderbilt and I was digging the marrons out of a Nesselrode when, presto, it suddenly came over me that the baroness was right and that *I could never marry a foreigner.* It came like a thunderclap. But somewhere in that senate of instinct which debates over such things down deep in the secret chambers of our souls, I suppose, the whole problem had been talked over and fought out and put to the vote. And in the face of the fact that Theobald Gustav had always seemed more nearly akin to one of Ouida's demigods than any man I had ever known, the vote had gone against him. My hero was no longer a hero. I knew there had been times, of course, when that hero, being a German, had rather regarded this universe of ours as a department-store and this earth as the particular section over which the August Master had appointed him floor-walker. I had thought of him as my *Eisenfresser* and my big blond *Saebierassler*. But my eyes opened with my last marron and I suddenly sat back and stared at Theobald's handsome pink face with its Krupp-steel blue eyes and its haughtily upturned mustache-ends. He must have seen that look of appraisal on my own face, for, with all his iron-and-blood Prussianism, he clouded up like a hurt child. But he was too much of a diplomat to show his feelings. He merely became so unctuously polite that I felt like poking him in his steel-blue eye with my mint straw.

Remember, Matilda Anne, not a word was said, not one syllable about what was there in both our souls. Yet it was one of life's biggest moments, the Great Divide of a whole career—and I went on eating Nesselrode and Theobald went on pleasantly smoking his cigarette and approvingly inspecting his well-manicured nails.

It was funny, but it made me feel blue and unattached and terribly alone in the world. Now, I can see things more clearly. I know that mood of mine was not the mere child of caprice. Looking back, I can see how Theobald had been more critical, more silently combative, from the moment I stepped off the *Baltic*. I realized, all at once, *that he had secretly been putting me to a strain*. I won't say it was because my *dot* had gone with The Nitrate Mines, or that he had discovered that Duncan had crossed on the same steamer with me, or that he knew I'd soon hear of the L—— episode. But these prophetic bones of mine told me there was trouble ahead. And I felt so forsaken and desolate in spirit that when Duncan whirled me out to Westbury, in a hired motor-car, to see the Great Neck First defeated by the Meadow Brook Hunters, I went with the happy-go-lucky glee of a truant who doesn't give a hang what happens. Dinky-Dunk was interested in polo ponies, which, he explained to me, are not a particular breed but just come along by accident—for he'd bred and sold mounts to the Coronado and San Mateo Clubs and the Philadelphia City Cavalry boys. And he loved the game. He was so genuine and sincere and *human*, as we sat there side by side, that I wasn't a bit afraid of him and knew we could be chums and didn't mind his lapses into silence or his extension-sole English shoes and crazy London cravat.

And I was happy, until the school-bell rang—which took the form of Theobald's telephone message to the Ritz reminding me of our dinner engagement. It was an awful dinner, for intuitively I knew what was coming, and quite as intuitively he knew what was coming, and even the waiter knew when it came,—for I flung Theobald's ring right against his stately German chest. There'd be no good in telling you, Matilda Anne, what led up to that most unlady-like action. I don't intend to burn incense in front of myself. It may have looked wrong. But I know you'll take my word when I say he deserved it. The one thing that hurts is that he had the triumph of being the first to sever diplomatic relations. In the language of Shorty McCabe and my fellow countrymen, *he threw me down!* Twenty minutes later, after composing my soul and powdering my nose, I was telephoning all over the city trying to find Duncan. I got him at last, and he came to the Ritz on the run. Then we picked up a residuary old horse-hansom on Fifth Avenue and went rattling off through Central Park. There I—who once boasted of seven proposals and three times that number of nibbles—promptly and shamelessly proposed to my Dinky-Dunk, though he is too much of a gentleman not to swear it's a horrid lie and that he'd have fought through an acre of Greek fire to get me!

But whatever happened, Count Theobald Gustav Von Guntner threw me down, and Dinky-Dunk caught me on the bounce, and now instead of going to embassy balls and talking world-politics like a Mrs. Humphry Ward heroine I've married a shack-owner who grows wheat up in the Canadian Northwest. And instead of wearing a tiara in the Grand Tier at the Metropolitan I'm up here a dot on the prairie and wearing an apron made of butcher's linen! *Sursum corda!* For I'm still in the ring. And it's no easy thing to fall in love and land on your feet. But I've gone and done it. I've taken the high jump. I've made my bed, as Uncle Carlton had the nerve to tell me, and now I've got to lie in it. But *assez d'Etrangers!*

That wedding-day of mine I'll always remember as a day of smells, the smell of the pew-cushions in the empty church, the smell of the lilies-of-the-valley, that dear, sweet, scatter-brained Fanny-Rain-In-The-Face (she rushed to town an hour after getting my wire) insisted on carrying, the smell of the leather in the damp taxi, the tobaccoy smell of Dinky-Dunk's quite impossible best man, who'd been picked up at the hotel, on the fly, to act as a witness, and the smell of Dinky-Dunk's brand new gloves as he lifted my chin and kissed me in that slow, tender, tragic, end-of-the-world way big and bashful men sometimes have with women. It's all a jumble of smells.

Then Dinky-Dunk got the wire saying he might lose his chance on the Stuart Ranch, if he didn't close before the Calgary interests got hold of it. And Dinky-Dunk wanted that ranch. So we talked it over and in five minutes had given up the idea of going down to Aiken and were telephoning for the stateroom on the Montreal Express. I had just four hours for shopping, scurrying about after cook-books and golf-boots and table-linen and a chafing dish, and a lot of other absurd things I thought we'd need on the ranch. And then off we flew for the West, before poor, extravagant, ecstatic Dinky-Dunk's thirty-six wedding orchids' from Thorley's had faded and before I'd a chance to show Fanny my nighties!

Am I crazy? Is it all wrong? Do I love my Dinky-Dunk? *Do* I? The Good Lord only knows, Matilda Anne! O God, O God, if it *should* turn out that I don't, that I can't? But I'm going to! I know I'm going to! And there's one other thing that I know, and when I remember it, it sends a comfy warm wave through all my body: Dinky-Dunk loves me. He's as mad as a hatter about me. He deserves to be loved back. And I'm going to love him back. That is a vow I herewith duly register. *I'm going to love my Dinky-Dunk*. But, oh, isn't it wonderful to wake love in a man, in a strong man? To be able to sweep him off, that way, on a tidal wave that leaves him rather white and shaky in the voice and trembly in the fingers, and seems to light a little luminous fire at the back of his eyeballs so that you can see the pupils glow, the same as an animal's when your motor head-lights hit them! It's like taking a little match and starting a prairie-fire and watching the flames creep and spread until the heavens are roaring! I wonder if I'm selfish? I wonder? But I can't answer that now, for it's supper time, and your Tabby has the grub to rustle!

Saturday the Twenty-first

I'm alone in the shack to-night, and I'm determined not to think about my troubles. So I'm going to write you a ream, Matilda Anne, whether you like it or not. And I must begin by telling you about the shack itself, and how I got here. All the way out from Montreal Dinky-Dunk, in his kindly way, kept doing his best to key me down and make me not expect too much. But I'd hold his hand, under the magazine I was pretending to read, and whistle *Home, Sweet Home*! He kept saying it would be hard, for the first year or two, and there would be a terrible number of things I'd be sure to miss. *Love Me and The World Is Mine!* I hummed, as I leaned over against his big wide shoulder. And I lay there smiling and happy, blind to everything that was before me, and I only laughed when Dinky-Dunk asked me if I'd still say that when I found there wasn't a nutmeg-grater within seven miles of my kitchen.

"Do you love me?" I demanded, hanging on to him right in front of the car-porter.

"I love you better than anything else in all this wide world!" was his slow and solemn answer.

When we left Winnipeg, too, he tried to tell me what a plain little shack we'd have to put up with for a year or two, and how it wouldn't be much better than camping out, and how he knew I was clear grit and would help him win that first year's battle. There was nothing depressing to me in the thought of life in a prairie-shack. I never knew, of course, just what it would be like, and had no way of knowing. I remembered Chinkie's little love of a farm in Sussex, and I'd been a week at the Westbury's place out on Long Island, with its terraced lawns and gardens and greenhouses and macadamized roads. And, on the whole, I expected a cross between a shooting-box and a Swiss chalet, a little nest of a home that was so small it was sure to be lovable, with a rambler-rose draping the front and a crystal spring bubbling at the back door, a little flowery island on the prairie where we could play Swiss-Family-Robinson and sally forth to shoot prairie-chicken and ruffed grouse to our hearts' content.

Well, that shack wasn't quite what I expected! But I mustn't run ahead of my story, Matilda Anne, so I'll go back to where Dinky-Dunk and I got off the side-line "accommodation" at Buckhorn, with our traps and trunks and hand-bags and suitcases. And these had scarcely been piled on the wooden platform before the station-agent came running up to Duncan with a yellow sheet in his hand. And Duncan looked worried as he read it, and stopped talking to his man called Olie, who was there beside the platform, in a big, sweat-stained Stetson hat, with a big team hitched to a big wagon with straw in the bottom of the box.

Olie, I at once told myself, was a Swede. He was one of the ugliest men I ever clapped eyes on, but I found out afterward that his face had been frozen in a blizzard, years before, and his nose had split. This had disfigured him—and the job had been done for life. His eyes were big and pale blue, and his hair and eyebrows were a pale yellow. He was the most silent man I ever saw. But Dinky-Dunk had already told me he was a great worker, and a fine fellow at heart. And when Dinky-Dunk says he'd trust a man, through thick and thin, there must be something good in that man, no matter how bulbous his nose is or how scared-looking he gets when a woman speaks to him. Olie looked more scared than ever when Dinky-Dunk suddenly ran to where the train-conductor was standing beside his car-steps, asked him to hold that "accommodation" for half a minute, pulled his suit-case from under my pile of traps, and grabbed little me in his arms.

"Quick," he said, "good-by! I've got to go on to Calgary. There's trouble about my registrations."

I hung on to him for dear life. "You're not going to leave me here, Dinky-Dunk, in the middle of this wilderness?" I cried out, while the conductor and brakeman and station-agent all called and hollooed and clamored for Duncan to hurry.

"Olie will take you home, beloved," Dinky-Dunk tried to assure me. "You'll be there by midnight, and I'll be back by Saturday evening!"

I began to bawl. "Don't go! Don't leave me!" I begged him. But the conductor simply tore him out of my arms and pushed him aboard the tail-end of the last car. I made a face at a fat man who was looking out a window at me. I stood there, as the train started to move, feeling that it was dragging my heart with it.

Then Dinky-Dunk called out to Olie, from the back platform: "Did you get my message and paint that shack?" And Olie, with my steamer-rug in his hand, only looked blank and called back "No." But I don't believe Dinky-Dunk even heard him, for he was busy throwing kisses at me. I stood there, at the edge of the platform, watching that lonely last car-end fade down into the lonely sky-line. Then I mopped my eyes, took one long quavery breath, and said out loud, as Birdalone Pebbley said Shiner did when he was lying wounded on the field of Magersfontein: "*Squealer, squealer, who's a squealer?*"

I found the big wagon-box filled with our things and Olie sitting there waiting, viewing me with wordless yet respectful awe. Olie, in fact, has never yet got used to me. He's a fine chap, in his rough and inarticulate way, and there's nothing he wouldn't do for me. But I'm a novelty to him. His pale blue eyes look frightened and he blushes when I speak to him. And he studies me secretly, as though I were a dromedary, or an archangel, or a mechanical toy whose inner mechanism perplexed him. But yesterday I found out through Dinky-Dunk what the probable secret of Olie's mystification was. It was my hat. "It ban so dam' foolish!" he fervently confessed.

That wagon-ride from Buckhorn out to the ranch seemed endless. I thought we were trekking clear up to the North Pole. At first there was what you might call a road, straight and worn deep, between parallel lines of barb-wire fencing. But this road soon melted into nothing more than a trail, a never-ending gently curving trail that ribboned out across the prairie-floor as far as the eye could see. It was a glorious afternoon, one of those opaline, blue-arched autumn days when it should have been a joy merely to be alive. But I was in an antagonistic mood, and the little cabin-like farmhouses that every now and then stood up against the sky-line made me feel lonesome, and the jolting of the heavy wagon made me tired, and by six o'clock I was so hungry that my ribs ached. We had been on the trail then almost five hours, and Olie calmly informed me it was only a few hours more. It got quite cool as the sun went down, and I had to undo my steamer-rug and get wrapped up in it. And still we went on. It seemed like being at sea, with a light now and then, miles and miles away. Something howled dismally in the distance, and gave me the creeps. Olie told me it was only a coyote. But we kept on, and my ribs ached worse than ever.

Then I gave a shout that nearly frightened Olie off the seat, for I remembered the box of chocolates we'd had on the train. We stopped and found my hand-bag, and lighted matches and looked through it. Then I gave a second and more dismal shout, for I remembered Dinky-Dunk had crammed it into his suit-case at the last moment. Then we went on again, with me a squaw-woman all wrapped in her blanket. I must have fallen asleep, for I woke with a start. Olie had stopped at a slough to water his team, and said we'd make home in another hour or two. How he found his way across that prairie Heaven only knows. I no longer worried. I was too tired to think. The open air and the swaying and jolting had chloroformed me into insensibility. Olie could have driven over the edge of a canyon and I should never have stopped him.

Instead of falling into a canyon, however, at exactly ten minutes to twelve we pulled up beside the shack door, which had been left unlocked, and Olie went in and lighted a lamp and touched a match to the fire already laid in the stove. I don't remember getting down from the wagon seat and I don't remember going into the shack. But when Olie came from putting in his team I was fast asleep on a luxurious divan made of a rather smelly steer-hide stretched across two slim cedar-trees on four little cedar legs, with a bag full of pine needles at the head. I lay there watching Olie, in a sort of torpor. It surprised me how quickly his big ungainly body could move, and how adept those big sunburned hands of his could be.

Then sharp as an arrow through a velvet curtain came the smell of bacon through my drowsiness. And it was a heavenly odor. I didn't even wash. I ate bacon and eggs and toasted biscuits and orange marmalade and coffee, the latter with condensed milk, which I hate. I don't know how I got to my bed, or got my clothes off, or where the worthy Olie slept, or who put out the light, or if the door had been left open or shut. I never knew that the bed was hard, or that the coyotes were howling. I only know that I slept for ten solid hours, without turning over, and that when I opened my eyes I saw a big square of golden sunlight dancing on the unpainted pine boards of the shack wall. And the funny part of it all was, Matilda Anne, I didn't have the splitting headache I'd so dolorously prophesied for myself. Instead of that I felt buoyant. I started to sing as I pulled on my stockings. And I suddenly remembered that I was terribly hungry again.

I swung open the window beside me, for it was on hinges, and poked my head out. I could see a corral, and a long low building which I took to be the ranch stables, and another and newer-looking building with a metal roof, and several stacks of hay surrounded by a fence, and a row of portable granaries. And beyond these stretched the open prairie, limitless and beautiful in the clear morning sunshine. Above it arched a sky of robin-egg blue, melting into opal and pale gold down toward the rim of the world. I breathed in lungfuls of clear, dry, ozonic air, and I really believe it made me a little light-headed, it was so exhilarating, so champagnized with the invisible bubbles of life.

I needed that etheric eye-opener, Matilda Anne, before I calmly and critically looked about our shack. Oh, that shack, that shack! What a comedown it was for your heart-sore Chaddie! In the first place, it seemed no bigger than a ship's cabin, and not one-half so orderly. It is made of lumber, and not of logs, and is about twelve feet wide and eighteen feet long. It has three windows, on hinges, and only one door. The floor is rather rough, and has a trap door leading into a small cellar, where vegetables can be stored for winter use. The end of the shack is shut off by a "tarp"—which I have just found out is short for tarpaulin. In other words, the privacy of my bedroom is assured by nothing more substantial than a canvas drop-curtain, shutting off my boudoir, where I could never very successfully *bouder*, from the larger living-room.

This living-room is also the kitchen, the laundry, the sewing-room, the reception-room and the library. It has a good big cookstove, which burns either wood or coal, a built-in cupboard with an array of unspeakably ugly crockery dishes, a row of shelves for holding canned goods, books and magazines, cooking utensils, gun-cartridges, tobacco-jars, carpenter's tools and a coal-oil lamp. There is also a plain pine table, a few chairs, one rocking-chair which has plainly been made by hand, and a flour-barrel. Outside the door is a wide wooden bench on which stands a big tin wash-basin and a cake of soap in a sardine can that has been punched full of holes along the bottom. Above it hung a roller towel which looked a little the worse for wear. And that was to be my home, my one and only habitation, for years and years to come! That little cat-eyed cubby-hole of a place!

I sat down on an overturned wash-tub about twenty paces from the shack, and studied it with calm and thoughtful eyes. It looked infinitely worse from the outside. The reason for this was that the board siding had first been covered with tar-paper, for the sake of warmth, and over this had been nailed pieces of tin, tin of every color and size and description. Some of it was flattened out stove-pipe, and some was obviously the sides of tomato-cans. Even tin tobacco-boxes and Dundee marmalade holders and the bottoms of old bake-pans and the sides of an old wash-boiler had been pieced together and patiently tacked over those shack-sides. It must have taken weeks and weeks to do. And it suddenly impressed me as something poignant, as something with the Vergilian touch of tears in it. It seemed so full of history, so vocal of the tragic expedients to which men on the prairie must turn. It seemed pathetic. It brought a lump into my throat. Yet that Joseph's Coat of metal was a neatly done bit of work. All it needed was a coat of paint or two, and it would look less like a crazy-quilt solidified into a homestead. And I suddenly remembered Dinky-Dunk's question called out to Olie from the car-end—and I knew he'd hurried off a message to have that telltale tinning-job painted over before I happened to clap eyes on it.

As Olie had disappeared from the scene and was nowhere to be found, I went in and got my own breakfast. It was supper over again, only I scrambled my eggs instead of frying them. And all the while I was eating that meal I studied those shack-walls and made mental note of what should be changed and what should be done. There was so much, that it rather overwhelmed me. I sat at the table, littered with its dirty dishes, wondering where to begin. And then the endless vista of it all suddenly opened up before me. I became nervously conscious of the unbroken silence about me, and I realized how different this new life must be from the old. It seemed like death itself, and it got a strangle hold on my nerves, and I knew

I was going to make a fool of myself the very first morning in my new home, in my home and Dinky-Dunk's. But I refused to give in. I did something which startled me a little, something which I had not done for years. I got down on my knees beside that plain wooden chair and prayed to God. I asked Him to give me strength to keep me from being a piker and make me a wife worthy of the man who loved me, and lead me into the way of bringing happiness to the home that was to be ours. Then I rolled up my sleeves, tied a face towel over my head and went to work.

It was a royal cleaning-out, I can tell you. In the afternoon I had Olie down on all fours scrubbing the floor. When he had washed the windows I had him get a garden rake and clear away the rubbish that littered the dooryard. I draped chintz curtains over the windows, and had Olie nail two shelves in a packing-box and then carry it into my boudoir behind the drop-curtain. Over this box I tacked fresh chintz (for the shack did not possess so feminine a thing as a dresser) and on it put my folding-mirror and my Tiffany traveling-clock and all my foolish shimmery silver toilet articles. Then I tacked up photographs and magazine-prints about the bare wooden walls—and decided that before the winter came those walls would be painted and papered, or I'd know the reason why. Then I aired the bedding and mattress, and unpacked my brand-new linen sheets and the ridiculous hemstitched pillow-slips that I'd scurried so frenziedly about the city to get, and stowed my things away on the box-shelves, and had Olie pound the life out of the well-sunned pillows, and carefully remade the bed.

And then I went at the living-room. And it was no easy task, reorganizing those awful shelves and making sure I wasn't throwing away things Dinky-Dunk might want later on. But the carnage was great, and all afternoon the smoke went heavenward from my fires of destruction. And when it was over I told Olie to go out for a good long walk, for I intended to take a bath. Which I did in the wash-tub, with much joy and my last cake of Roger-and-Gallet soap. And I had to shout to poor ambulating Olie for half-an-hour before I could persuade him to come in to supper. And even then he came tardily, with countless hesitations and pauses, as though a lady temerarious enough to take a scrub were for all time taboo to the race of man. And when he finally ventured in through the door, round-eyed and blushing a deep russet, he gaped at my white middy and my little white apron with that silent but eloquent admiration which couldn't fail to warm the cockles of the most unimpressionable housewife's heart.

Monday the Twenty-third

My Dinky-Dunk is back—and oh, the difference to me! I kept telling myself that I was too busy to miss him. He came Saturday night as I was getting ready for bed. I'd been watching the trail every now and then, all day long, and by nine o'clock had given him up. When I heard him shouting for Olie, I made a rush for him, with only half my clothes on, and nearly shocked Olie and some unknown man, who'd driven Dinky-Dunk home, to death. How I hugged my husband! My husband—I love to write that word. And when I got him inside we had it all over again. He was just like a big overgrown boy. And he put the table between us, so he'd have a chance to talk. But even that didn't work. He smothered my laughing in kisses, and held me up close to him and said I was wonderful. Then we'd try to get down to earth again, and talk sensibly, and then there'd be another death-clinch. Dinky-Dunk says I'm worse than he is. "Of course it's all up with a man," he confessed, "when he sees you coming for him with that Australian crawl-stroke of yours!"

For which I did my best to break in his floating ribs. Heaven only knows how late we talked that night. And Dinky-Dunk had a bundle of surprises for me. The first was a bronze reading-lamp. The second was a soft little rug for the bedroom—only an Axminster, but very acceptable. The third was a pair of Juliets, lined with fur, and oceans too big for me. And Dinky-Dunk says by Tuesday we'll have two milk-cows, part-Jersey, at the ranch, and inside of a week a crate of hens will be ours. Thereupon I couldn't help leading Duncan to the inventory I had made of what we had, and the list, on the opposite side, of what we had to have. The second thing under the heading of "Needs" was "lamp," the fifth was "bedroom rug," the thirteenth was "hens," and the next was "cow." I think he was rather amazed at the length of that list of "needs," but he says I shall have everything in reason. And when he kind of settled down, and noticed the changes in the living-room and then went in and inspected the bedroom he grew very solemn, of a sudden. It worried me.

"Lady Bird," he said, taking me in his arms, "this is a pretty hard life I've trapped you into. It will *have* to be hard for a year or two, but we'll win out, in the end, and I guess it'll be worth the fight!"

Dinky-Dunk is such a dear. I told him of course we'd win out, but I wouldn't be much use to him at first. I'd have to get broken in and made bridle-wise.

"But, oh, Dinky-Dunk, whatever happens, you must always love me!"—and I imagine I swam for him with my Australian crawl-stroke again. All I remember is that we went to sleep in each other's arms. And as I started to say and forgot to finish, I'd been missing my Dinky-Dunk more than I imagined, those last few days. After that night it was no longer just a shack. It was "Home." Home—it's such a beautiful word! It must mean so much to every woman. And I fell asleep telling myself it was the loveliest word in the English language.

In the morning I slipped out of bed before Dinky-Dunk was awake, for breakfast was to be our first home meal, and I wanted it to be a respectable one. *Der Mensch ist was er isst*—so I must feed my lord and master on the best in the land. Accordingly I put an extra tablespoonful of cream in the scrambled eggs, and two whole eggs in the coffee, to make dead sure it was crystal-clear. Then, feeling like Van Roon when Berlin declared war on France, I rooted out Dinky-Dunk, made him wash, and sat him down in his pajamas and his ragged old dressing-gown.

"I suppose," I said as I saw his eyes wander about the table, "that you feel exactly like an oyster-man who's just chipped his Blue-Point and got his knife-edge in under the shell! And the next wrench is going to tell you exactly what sort of an oyster you've got!"

Dinky-Dunk grinned up at me as I buttered his toast, piping hot from the range. "Well, Lady Bird, you're not the kind that'll need paprika, anyway!" he announced as he fell to. And he ate like a boa-constrictor and patted his pajama-front and stentoriously announced that he'd picked a queen—only he pronounced it kaveen, after the manner of our poor old Swedish Olie!

As that was Sunday we spent the morning "pi-rooting" about the place. Dinky-Dunk took me out and showed me the stables and the hay-stacks and the granaries—which he'd just waterproofed so there'd be no more spoilt grain on that farm—and the "cool-hole" he used to use before the cellar was built, and the ruins of the sod-hut where the first homesteader that owned that land had lived. Then he showed me the new bunk-house for the men, which Olie is finishing in his spare time. It looks much better than our own shack, being of planed lumber. But Dinky-Dunk is loyal to the shack, and says it's really better built, and the warmest shack in the West—as I'll find before winter is over.

Then we stopped at the pump, and Dinky-Dunk made a confession. When he first bought that ranch there was no water at the shack, except what he could catch from the roof. Water had to be hauled for miles, and it was muddy and salty, at that. They used to call it "Gopher soup." This lack of water always worried him, he said, for women always want water, and oodles of it. It was the year before, after he had left me at Banff, that he was determined to get water. It was hard work, putting down that well, and up to almost the last moment it promised to be a dry hole. But when they struck that water, Dinky-Dunk says, he decided in his soul that he was going to have me, if I was to be had. It was water fit for a queen. And he wanted his queen. But of course even queens have to be well laved and well laundered. He said he didn't sleep all night, after they found the water was there. He was too happy; he just went meandering about the prairie, singing to himself.

"So you were pretty sure of me, Kitten-Cats, even then?" I demanded.

He looked at me with his solemn Scotch-Canadian eyes. "I'm not sure of you, even now," was his answer. But I made him take it back.

It's rather odd how Dinky-Dunk got this ranch, which used to be called the Cochrane Ranch, for even behind this peaceful little home of ours there is a touch of tragedy. Hugh Cochrane was one of Dinky-Dunk's surveyors when he first took up railroad work in British Columbia. Hugh had a younger brother Andrew, who was rather wild and had been brought out here and planted on the prairie to keep him out of mischief. One winter night he rode nearly thirty miles to a dance (they do that apparently out here, and think nothing of it) and instead of riding home at five o'clock in the morning, with the others, he visited a whisky-runner who was operating a "blind pig." There he acquired much more whisky than was good for him and got lost on the trail. That meant he was badly frozen and probably out of his mind before he got back to the shack. He wasn't able to keep up a fire, of course, or do anything for himself—and I suppose the poor boy simply froze to death. He was alone there, and it was weeks and weeks before his body was found. But the most gruesome part of it all is that his horses had been stabled, tied up in their stalls without feed. They were all found dead, poor brutes. They'd even eaten the wooden boards the mangers were built of. Hugh Cochrane couldn't get over it, and was going to sell the ranch for fourteen hundred dollars when Dinky-Dunk heard of it and stepped in and bought the whole half-section. Then he bought the McKinnon place, a half-section to the north of this, after McKinnon had lost all his buildings because he was too shiftless to make a fire-guard. And when the railway work was finished Dinky-Dunk took up wheat-growing. He is a great believer in wheat. He says wheat spells wealth, in this country. Some people call him a "land-miner," he says, but when he's given the chance to do the thing as he wants to, he'll show them who's right.

Wednesday the Twenty-fifth

Dinky-Dunk and I have been making plans. He's promised to build an annex to the shack, a wing on the north side, so I can have a store-room and a clothes-closet at one end and a guest-chamber at the other. And I'm to have a sewing-machine and a bread-mixer, and the smelly steer-hide divan is going to be banished to the bunk-house. And Dinky-Dunk says I must have a pinto, a riding-horse, as soon as he can lay hands on the right animal. Later on he says I must have help, but out here in the West women are hard to get, and harder to keep. They are snatched up by lonely bachelors like Dinky-Dunk. They can't even keep the school-teachers (mostly girls from Ontario) from marrying off. But I don't want a woman about, not for a few months yet. I want Dinky-Dunk all to myself. And the freedom of isolation like this is such a luxury! To be just one's self, in civilization, is a luxury, is the greatest luxury in the world,—and also the most expensive, I've found to my sorrow.

Out here, there's no object in being anything but one's self. Life is so simple and honest, so back to first principles! There's joy in the thought of getting rid of all the sublimated junk of city life. I'm just a woman; and Dinky-Dunk is just a man. We've got a roof and a bed and a fire. That's all. And what is there, really, after that? We have to eat, of course, but we really live well. There's all the game we want, especially wild duck and prairie chicken, to say nothing of jack-rabbit. Dinky-Dunk sallies out and pots them as we need them. We get our veal and beef by the quarter, but it will not keep well until the weather gets cooler, so I put what we don't need in brine and use it for boiling-meat. We have no fresh fruit, but even evaporated peaches can be stewed so that they're appetizing. And as I had the good sense to bring out with me no less than three cook-books, from Brentano's, I am able to attempt more and more elaborate dishes.

Olie has a wire-fenced square where he grew beets and carrots and onions and turnips, and the biggest potatoes I ever saw. These will be pitted before the heavy frosts come. We get our butter and lard by the pail, and our flour by the sack, but getting things in quantities sometimes has its drawbacks. When I examined the oatmeal box I found it had weavels in it, and promptly threw all that meal away. Dinky-Dunk, coming in from the corral, viewed the pile with round-eyed amazement. "It's got *worms* in it!" I cried out to him. He took up a handful of it, and stared at it with tragic sorrow. "Why, I ate weavels all last winter," he reprovingly remarked. Dinky-Dunk, with his Scotch strain, loves his porridge. So we'll have to get a hundred-weight, guaranteed strictly uninhabited, when we team into Buckhorn.

Men are funny! A woman never quite knows a man until she has lived with him and day by day unearthed his little idiosyncrasies. She may seem close to him, in those earlier days of romance, but she never really knows him, any more than a sparrow on a telegraph wire knows the Morse Code thrilling along under its toes! Men have so many little kinks and turns, even the best of them. I tacked oil-cloth on a shoe-box and draped chintz around it, and fixed a place for Dinky-Dunk to wash, in the bedroom, when he comes in at noon. At night I knew it would be impossible, for he's built a little wash-house with old binder-carrier canvas nailed to four posts, and out there Olie and he strip every evening and splash each other with horse-pails full of well-water. Dinky-Dunk is clean, whatever he may be, but I thought it would look more civilized if he'd perform his limited noonday ablutions in the bedroom. He did it for one day, in pensive silence, and then sneaked the wash-things back to the rickety old bench outside the door. He said it saved time.

Among other vital things, I've found that Dinky-Dunk hates burnt toast. Yesterday morning, Matilda Anne, I got thinking about Corfu and Ragusa and you, and it *did* burn a little around the edges, I suppose. So I kissed his ear and told him carbon would make his teeth white. But he got up and went out with a sort of "In-this-way-madness-lies" expression, and I felt wretched all day. So this morning I was more careful. I did that toast just to a turn. "Feast, O Kaikobád, on the blondest of toast!" I said as I salaamed and handed him the plate. He wrinkled up his forehead a little, at the sting in that speech, but he could not keep from grinning. Then, too, Dinky-Dunk always soaps the back of his hand, to wash his back, and reach high up. So do I. And on cold mornings-he says "One, two, three, the bumble bee!" before he hops out of bed—and I imagined I was the only grownup in all the wide world who still made use of that foolish rhyme. And the other day when he was hot and tired I found him drinking a dipperful of cold water fresh from the well. So I said:

"Many a man has gone to his sarcophagusThro' pouring cold water down a warm esophagus!"

When I recited that rhyme to him he swung about as though he'd been shot. "Where did you ever hear that?" he asked. I told him that was what Lady Agatha always said to me when she caught me drinking ice-water. "I thought I was the only man in the world who knew that crazy old couplet," he confessed, and he chased me around the shack with the rest of the dipperful, to keep from chilling his tummy, he explained. Then Dinky-Dunk and I both like to give pet-names to things. He calls me "Lady Bird" and "Gee-Gee" and sometimes "Honey," and sometimes "Boca Chica" and "Tabby." And I call him Dinky-Dunk and The Dour Maun, and Kitten-Cats, though for some reason or other he hates that last name. I think he feels it's an affront to his dignity. And no man likes a trace of mockery in a woman. But Dinky-Dunk's names are born of affection, and I love him for them.

Even the ranch horses have all been tagged with names. There's "Slip-Along" and "Water Light" and "Bronk" and "Patsy Crocker" and "Pick and Shovel" and "Tumble Weed," and others that I can't remember at the moment. And I find I'm picking up certain of Dinky-Dunk's little habits, and dropping into the trick of looking at things from his standpoint. I wonder if husbands and wives really *do* get to be alike? There are times when Dinky-Dunk seems to know just what I'm thinking, for when he speaks he says exactly the thing I was going to ask him. And he's inexorable in his belief that one's right shoe should always be put on first. So am I!

Thursday the Twenty-sixth

Dinky-Dunk is rather pinched for ready money. He is what they call "land poor" out here. He has big plans, but not much cash. So we shall have to be frugal. I had decided on vast and sudden changes in this household, but I'll have to draw in my horns a little. Luckily I have nearly two hundred dollars of my own money left—and have never mentioned it to Dinky-Dunk. So almost every night I study the magazine advertisements, and the catalog of the mail-order house in Winnipeg. Each night I add to my list of "Needs," and then go back and cross out some of the earlier ones, as being too extravagant, for the length of my list almost gives me heart-failure. And as I sit there thinking of what I have to do without, I envy the women I've known in other days, the women with all their white linen and their cut glass and silverware and their prayer-rugs and period rooms and their white-tiled baths and their machinery for making life so comfortable and so easy. I envy them. I put away my list, and go to bed envying them. But, oh, I sleep so soundly, and I wake up so buoyant in heart, so eager to get at the next day's work, so glad to see I'm slowly getting things more ship-shape. It doesn't leave room for regret. And there is always the future, the happier to-morrow to which our thoughts go out. I get to thinking of the city again, of the hundreds of women I know going like hundreds of crazy squirrels on their crazy treadmill of amusements, and of the thousands and thousands of women who are toiling without hope, going on in the same old rut from day to day, cooped up in little flats and back rooms, with bad air and bad food and bad circulation, while I have all God's outdoors to wander about in, and can feel the singing rivers of health in my veins. And here I side-step my Song-of-Solomon voluntary, for they have one thing I *do* miss, and that is music. I wish I had a cottage-piano or a Baby Grand or a *Welte Mignon*! I wish I had any kind of an old piano! I wish I had an accordion, or a German Sweet-Potato, or even a Jew's-Harp!

But what's the use of wishing for luxuries, when we haven't even a can-opener—Dinky-Dunk says he's used a hatchet for over a year! And our only toaster is a kitchen-fork wired to the end of a lath. I even saw Dinky-Dunk spend half an hour straightening out old nails taken from one of our shipping-boxes. And the only colander we have was made out of a leaky milk-pan with holes punched in its bottom. And we haven't a double-boiler or a mixing-bowl or a doughnut-cutter. When I told Dinky-Dunk yesterday that we were running out of soap, he said he'd build a leach of wood-ashes and get beef-tallow and make soft soap. I asked him how long he'd want to kiss a downy cheek that had been washed in soft soap. He said he'd keep on kissing me if I was a mummy pickled in bitumen. But I prefer not risking too much of the pickling process.

Which reminds me of the fact that I find my hair a terrible nuisance, with no Hortense to struggle with it every morning. As you know, it's as thick as a rope and as long as my arm. I begrudge the time it takes to look after it, and such a thing as a good shampoo is an event to be approached with trepidation and prepared for with zeal. "Coises on me beauty!" I think I'll cut that wool off. But on each occasion when I have my mind about made up I experience one of "Mr. Polly's" l'il dog moments. The thing that makes me hesitate is the thought that Dinky-Dunk might hate me for the rest of his days. And now that our department-store aristocracy seems to have a corner in Counts and I seem destined to worry along with merely an American husband, I don't intend to throw away the spoons with the dish-water! But having to fuss so with that hair is a nuisance, especially at night, when I am so tired that my pillow seems to bark like a dog for me to come and pat it.

And speaking of that reminds me that I have to order arch-supports for my feet. I'm on them so much that by bedtime my ankles feel like a *chocolat mousse* that's been left out in the sun. Yet this isn't a whimper, Matilda Anne, for when I turn in I sleep like a child. No more counting and going to the medicine-chest for coal-tar pills. I abjure them. I, who used to have so many tricks to bring the starry-eyed goddess bending over my pillow, hereby announce myself as the noblest sleeper north of the Line! I no longer need to count the sheep as they come over the wall, or patiently try to imagine the sound of surf-waves, or laboriously re-design that perennial dinner-gown which I've kept tucked away in the cedar-chest of the imagination as long as I can remember, elaborating it over and over again down to the minutest details through the longest hour of my whitest white night until it began to merge into the velvety robes of slumber itself! Nowadays an ogre called Ten-O'Clock steals up behind my chair with a club in his hand and stuns me into insensibility. Two or three times, in fact, my dear old clumsy-fingered Dinky-Dunk has helped me get my clothes off. But he says that the nicest sound he knows is to lie in bed and hear the tinkle of my hair-pins as I toss them into the little Coalport pin-tray on my dresser—which reminds me what Chinkie once said about his idea of Heaven being eating my divinity-fudge to the sound of trumpets!

I brag about being busy, but I'm not the only busy person about this wickyup. Olie and Dinky-Dunk talk about summer-fallowing and double-discing and drag-harrowing and fire-guarding, and I'm beginning to understand what it all means. They are out with their teams all day long, working like Trojans. We have mid-day dinner, which Olie bolts in silence and with the rapidity of chain-lightning. He is the most expert of sword-swallowers, with a table-knife, and Dinky-Dunk says it keeps reminding him how Burbank could make a fortune inventing a square pea that would stay on a knife-blade. But Dinky-Dunk stopped me calling him "The Sword Swallower" and has privately tipped Olie off as to the functions of the table fork. How the males of this old earth stick together! The world of men is a secret order, and every man is a member!

Having bolted his dinner Olie always makes for outdoors. Then Dinky-Dunk comes to my side of the table. We sit side by side, with our arms around each other. Sometimes I fill his pipe for him and light it. Then we talk lazily, happily, contentedly and sometimes shockingly. Then he looks at our nickel-alarm clock, up on the book shelves which I made out of old biscuit-boxes, and invariably says: "This isn't the spirit that built Rome," and kisses me three times, once on each eyelid, tight, and once on the mouth. I don't even mind the taste of the pipe. Then he's off, and I'm alone for the afternoon.

But I'm getting things organized now so that I have a little spare time. And with time on my hands I find myself turning very restless. Yesterday I wandered off on the prairie and nearly got lost. Dinky-Dunk says I must be more careful, until I get to know the country better. He put me up on his shoulder and made me promise. Then he let me down. It made me wonder if I hadn't married a masterful man. Above all things I've always wanted freedom.

"I'm a wild woman, Duncan. You'll never tame me," I confessed to him.

He laughed a little.

"So you think you will?" I demanded.

"No, *I* won't, Gee-Gee, but life will!"

And again I felt some ghostly spirit of revolt stirring in me, away down deep. I think he saw some shadow of it, caught some echo of it, for his manner changed and he pushed back the hair from my forehead and kissed me, almost pityingly.

"There's one thing must *not* happen!" I told him as he held me in his arms.

He did not let his eyes meet mine.

"Why?" he asked.

"I'm afraid—out here!" I confessed as I clung to him and felt the need of having him close to me. He was very quiet and thoughtful all evening. Before I fell asleep he told me that on Monday the two of us would team in to Buckhorn and get a wagon-load of supplies.

Saturday the Twenty-eighth

I have got my cayuse. Dinky-Dunk meant him for a surprise, but the shyest and reddest-headed cowboy that ever sat in a saddle came cantering along the trail, and I saw him first. He was leading the shaggiest, piebaldest, pottest-tummied, craziest-looking little cayuse that ever wore a bridle. I gave one look at his tawny-colored forelock, which stood pompadour-style about his ears, and shouted out "Paderewski!" Dinky-Dunk came and stood beside me and laughed. He said that cayuse *did* look like Paderewski, but the youth of the fiery locks blushingly explained that his present name was "Jail-Bird," which some fool Scandinavian had used instead of "Grey-Bird," his authentic and original appellative. But I stuck to my name, though we have shortened it into "Paddy." And Paddy must indeed have been a jail-bird, or deserved to be one, for he is marked and scarred from end to end. But he is good-tempered, tough as hickory and obligingly omnivorous. Every one in the West, men and women alike, rides astride, and I have been practising on Paddy. It seems a very comfortable and sensible way to ride, but I shall have to toughen up a bit before I hit the trail for any length of time.

I've been wondering, Matilda Anne, if this all sounds pagan and foolish to you, uncultured, as Theobald Gustav would put it? I've also been wondering, since I wrote that last sentence, if people really need culture, or what we used to call culture, and if it means as much to life as so many imagine. Here we are out here without any of the refinements of civilization, and we're as much at peace with our own souls as are the birds of the air—when there *are* birds in the air, which isn't in our country! Culture, it seems to me as I look back on things, tends to make people more and more mere spectators of life, detaching them from it and lifting them above it. Or can it be that the mere spectators demand culture, to take the place of what they miss by not being actual builders and workers?

We are farmers, just rubes and hicks, as they say in my country. But we're tilling the soil and growing wheat. We're making a great new country out of what was once a wilderness. To me, that seems almost enough. We're laboring to feed the world, since the world must have bread, and there's something satisfying and uplifting in the mere thought that we can answer to God, in the end, for our lives, no matter how raw and rude they may have been. And there are mornings when I am Browning's "Saul" in the flesh. The great wash of air from sky-line to sky-line puts something into my blood or brain that leaves me almost dizzy. I sizzle! It makes me pulse and tingle and cry out that life is good—*good*! I suppose it is nothing more than altitude and ozone. But in the matter of intoxicants it stands on a par with anything that was ever poured out of bottles at Martin's or Bustanoby's. And at sunrise, when the prairie is thinly silvered with dew, when the tiny hammocks of the spider-webs swing a million sparkling webs strung with diamonds, when every blade of grass is a singing string of pearls, hymning to God on High for the birth of a golden day, I can feel my heart swell, and I'm so abundantly, so inexpressibly alive, alive to every finger-tip! Such space, such light, such distances! And being Saul is so much better than reading about him!

Wednesday the First

I was too tired to write any last night, though there seemed so much to talk about. We teamed into Buckhorn for our supplies, two leisurely, lovely, lazy days on the trail, which we turned into a sort of gipsy-holiday. We took blankets and grub and feed for the horses and a frying-pan, and camped out on the prairie. The night was pretty cool, but we made a good fire, and had hot coffee. Dinky-Dunk smoked and I sang. Then we rolled up in our blankets and as I lay there watching the stars I got thinking of the lights of the Great White Way. Then I nudged my husband and asked him if he knew what my greatest ambition in life used to be. And of course he didn't. "Well, Dinky-Dunk," I told him, "it was to be the boy who opens the door at *Malliard's*! For two whole years I ate my heart out with envy of that boy, who always lived in the odor of such heavenly hot chocolate and wore two rows of shining buttons down his braided coat and was never without white gloves and morning, noon and night paraded about in the duckiest little skull-cap cocked very much to one side like a Grenadier's!" And Dinky-Dunk told me to go to sleep or he'd smother me with a horse-blanket. So I squirmed back into my blanket and got "nested" and watched the fire die away while far, far off somewhere a coyote howled. That made me lonesome, so I got Dinky-Dunk's hand, and fell asleep holding it in mine.

I woke up early. Dinky-Dunk had forgotten about my hand, and it was cold. In the East there was a low bar of ethereally pale silver, which turned to amber, and then to ashes of roses, and then to gold. I saw one sublime white star go out, in the West, and then behind the bars of gold the sky grew rosy with morning until it was one Burgundian riot of bewildering color. I sat up and watched it. Then I reached over and shook Dinky-Dunk. It was too glorious a daybreak to miss. He looked at me with one eye open, like a sleepy hound.

"You must see it, Dinky-Dunk! It's so resplendent it's positively vulgar!"

He sat up, stared at the pageantry of color for one moment, and then wriggled down into his blanket again. I tickled his nose with a blade of sweet-grass. Then I washed my face in the dew, the same as we did in Christ-Church Meadow that glorious May-Day in Oxford. By the time Dinky-Dunk woke up I had the coffee boiling and the bacon sizzling in the pan. It was the most celestial smell that ever assailed human nostrils, and I blush with shame at the thought of how much I ate at that breakfast, sitting flat on an empty oat-sack and leaning against a wagon-wheel. By eight o'clock we were in the metropolis of Buckhorn and busy gathering up our things there. And they made a very respectable wagon-load.

Thursday the Second

I have been practising like mad learning to play the mouth-organ. I bought it in Buckhorn, without letting Dinky-Dunk know, and all day long, when I knew it was safe, I've been at it. So to-night, when I had my supper-table all ready, I got the ladder that leaned against one of the granaries and mounted the nearest hay-stack. There, quite out of sight, I waited until Dinky-Dunk came in with his team. I saw him go into the shack and then step outside again, staring about in a brown study. Then I struck up *Traumerei*.

You should have seen that boy's face! He looked up at the sky, as though my poor little harmonica were the aërial outpourings of archangels. He stood stock-still, drinking it in. Then he bolted for the stables, thinking it came from there. It took him some time to corner me up on my stack-top. Then I slid down into his arms. And I believe he loves that mouth-organ music. After supper he made me go out and sit on the oat-box and play my repertory. He says it's wonderful, from a distance. But that mouth-organ's rather brassy, and it makes my lips sore. Then, too, my mouth isn't big enough for me to "tongue" it properly. When I told Dinky-Dunk this he said:

"Of course it isn't! What d'you suppose I've been calling you Boca Chica for?"

And I've just discovered "Boca Chica" is Spanish for "Little Mouth"—and me with a trap, Matilda Anne, that you used to call the Cave of the Winds! Now Dinky-Dunk vows he'll have a Victrola before the winter is over! Ye gods and little fishes, what a luxury! There was a time, not so long ago, when I was rather inclined to sniff at the Westbury's electric player-piano and its cabinet of neatly canned classics! How life humbles us! And how blind all women are in their ideals and their search for happiness! The sea-stones that lie so bright on the shores of youth can dry so dull in the hand of experience! And yet, as Birdalone's Nannie once announced, "If you thuck 'em they thay boo-ful!" And I guess it must be a good deal the same with marriage. You can't even afford to lay down on your job of loving. The more we ask, the more we must give. I've just been thinking of those days of my fiercely careless childhood when my soul used to float out to placid happiness on one piece of plum-cake—only even then, alas, it floated out like a polar bear on its iceberg, for as that plum-cake vanished my peace of mind went with it, madly as I clung to the last crumb. But now that I'm an old married woman I don't intend to be a Hamlet in petticoats.

A good man loves me, and I love him back. And I intend to keep that love alive.

Friday the Third

I have just issued an ultimatum as to pigs. There shall be no more loose porkers wandering about my dooryard. It's an advertisement of bad management. And what's more, when I was hanging out my washing this morning a shote rooted through my basket of white clothes with his dirty nose, and while I made after him his big brother actually tried to eat one of my wet table-napkins. And that meant another hour's hard work before the damage was repaired.

Saturday the Fourth

Olie is painting the shack, inside and out, and now you'd never know our poor little Joseph-coat home. I told Dinky-Dunk if we'd ever put a chameleon on that shack-wall he'd have died of brain-fag trying to make good on the color-schemes. So Dinky-Dunk made Olie take a day off and ply the brush. But the smell of paint made me think of Channel passages, so off I went with Dinky-Dunk, *a la* team and buckboard, to the Dixon Ranch to see about some horses, nearly seventy miles there and back. It was a glorious autumn day, and a glorious ride, with "Bronk" and "Tumble-Weed" loping along the double-trail and the air like crystal.

Dinky-Dunk and I sang most of the way. The gophers must have thought we were mad. My lord and master is incontinently proud of his voice, especially the chest-tones, but he rather tails behind me on the tune, plainly not always being sure of himself. We had dinner with the Dixons, and about three million flies. They gave me the blues, that family, and especially Mrs. Dixon. She seemed to make prairie-life so ugly and empty and hardening. Poor, dried-up, sad-eyed soul, she looked like a woman of sixty, and yet her husband said she was just thirty-seven. Their water is strong with alkali, and this and the prairie wind (combined with a something deep down in her own make-up) have made her like a vulture, lean and scrawny and dry. I stared at that hard line of jaw and cheekbone and wondered how long ago the soft curves were there, and if those overworked hands had ever been pretty, and if that flat back had ever been rounded and dimpled. Her hair was untidy. Her apron was unspeakably dirty, and she used it as both a handkerchief and a hand-towel. Her voice was as hard as nails, and her cooking was wretched. Not a door or window was screened, and, as I said before, we were nearly smothered with flies.

Dinky-Dunk did not dare to look at me, all dinner time. And on the way home Mrs. Dixon's eyes kept haunting me, they seemed so tired and vacant and accusing, as though they were secretly holding God Himself to account for cheating her out of her woman's heritage of joy. I asked Dinky-Dunk if we'd ever get like that. He said, "Not on your life!" and quoted the Latin phrase about mind controlling matter. The Dixons, he went on to explain, were of the "slum" type, only they didn't happen to live in a city. But tired and sleepy as I was that night, I got up to cold-cream my face and arms. And I'm going to write for almond-meal and glycerin from the mail-order house to-morrow. *And* a brassiere—for I saw what looked like the suspicion of a smile on Dinky-Dunk's unshaven lips as he watched me struggling into my corsets this morning. It took some writhing, and even then I could hardly make it. I threw my wet sponge after him when he turned back in the doorway with the mildly impersonal question: "Who's your fat friend?" Then he scooted for the corral, and I went back and studied my chin in the dresser-mirror, to make sure it wasn't getting terraced into a dew-lap like Uncle Carlton's.

But I can't help thinking of the Dixons, and feeling foolishly and helplessly sorry for them. It was dusk when we got back from that long drive to their ranch, and the stars were coming out. I could see our shack from miles off, a little lonely dot of black against the sky-line. I made Dinky-Dunk stop the team, and we sat and looked at it. It seemed so tiny there, so lonely, so strange, in the middle of such miles and miles of emptiness, with a little rift of smoke going up from its desolate little pipe-end. Then I said, out loud, "Home! My home!" And out of a clear sky, for no earthly reason, I began to cry like a baby. Women are such fools, sometimes! I told Dinky-Dunk we must get books, good books, and spend the long winter evenings reading together, to keep from going to seed.

He said, "All right, Gee-Gee," and patted my knee. Then we loped on along the trail toward the lonely little black dot ahead of us. But I hung on to Dinky-Dunk's arm, all the rest of the way, until we pulled up beside the shack, and poor old Olie, with a frying-pan in his hand, stood silhouetted against the light of the open door.

Monday the Sixth

The last few days I've been nothing but a two-footed retriever, scurrying off and carrying things back home with me. There have been rains, but the weather is still glorious. And I've discovered such heaps and heaps of mushrooms over at the old Titchborne Ranch. They're thick all around the corral and in the pasture there. I am now what your English lord and master would call "a perfect seat" on Paddy, and every morning I ride over after my basketful of *Agaricus Campestris*—that ought to be in the plural, but I've forgotten how! We have them creamed on toast; we have them fried in butter; and we have them in soup—and such beauties! I'm going to try and can some for winter and spring use. But the finest part of the mushroom is the finding it. To ride into a little white city that has come up overnight and looks like an encampment of fairy soldiers, to see the milky white domes against the vivid green of the prairie-grass, to catch sight of another clump of them, suddenly, like stars against an emerald sky, a hundred yards away, to inhale the clean morning air, and feel your blood tingle, and hear the prairie-chickens whir and the wild-duck scolding along the coulee-edges—I tell you, Matilda Anne, it's worth losing a little of your beauty sleep to go through it! I'm awake even before Dinky-Dunk, and I brought him out of his dreams this morning by poking his teeth with my little finger and saying:

"Twelve white horsesOn a red hill—"

and I asked him if he knew what it was, and he gave the right answer, and said he hadn't heard that conundrum since he was a boy.

All afternoon I've been helping Dinky-Dunk put up a barb-wire fence. Barb-wire is nearly as hard as a woman to handle. Dinky-Dunk is fencing in some of the range, for a sort of cattle-run for our two milk-cows. He says it's only a small field, but there seemed to be miles and miles of that fencing. We had no stretcher, so Dinky-Dunk made shift with me and a claw-hammer. He'd catch the wire, lever his hammer about a post, and I'd drive in the staple, with a hammer of my own. I got so I could hit the staple almost every whack, though one staple went off like shrapnel and hit Diddum's ear. So I'm some use, you see, even if I am a chekako! But a wire slipped, and tore through my skirt and stocking, scratched my leg and made the blood run. It was only the tiniest cut, really, but I made the most of it, Dinky-Dunk was so adorably nice about doctoring me up. We came home tired and happy, singing together, and Olie, as usual, must have thought we'd both gone mad.

This husband of mine is so elementary. He secretly imagines that he's one of the most complex of men. But in a good many things he's as simple as a child. And I love him for it, although I believe I *do* like to bedevil him a little. He is dignified, and hates flippancy. So when I greet him with "Morning, old boy!" I can see that nameless little shadow sweep over his face. Then I say, "Oh, I beg its little pardon!" He generally grins, in the end, and I think I'm slowly shaking that monitorial air out of him, though once or twice I've had to remind him about La Rochefoucauld saying gravity was a stratagem invented to conceal the poverty of the mind! But Dinky-Dunk still objects to me putting my finger on his Adam's apple when he's talking. He wears a flannel shirt, when working outside, and his neck is bare. Yesterday I buried my face down in the corner next to his shoulder-blade and made him wriggle. As he shaves only on Sunday mornings now, that is about the only soft spot, for his face is prickly, and makes my chin sore, the bearded brute! Then I bit him; not hard—but Satan said bite, and I just had to do it. He turned quite pale, swung me round so that I lay limp in his arms, and closed his mouth over mine. I got away, and he chased me. We upset things. Then I got outside the shack, ran around the horse-corral, and then around the hay-stacks, with Dinky-Dunk right after me, giving me goose-flesh at every turn. I felt like a cave-woman. He grabbed me like a stone-age man and caught me up and carried me over his shoulder to a pile of prairie sweet-grass that had been left there for Olie's mattress. My hair was down. I was screaming, half sobbing and half laughing. He dropped me in the hay, like a bag of wheat. I started to fight him again. But I couldn't beat him off. Then all my strength seemed to go. He was laughing himself, but it frightened me a little to see his pupils so big that his eyes looked black. I felt like a lamb in a lion's jaw, Dinky-Dunk is so much stronger than I am. I lay there quite still, with my eyes closed. I went flop. I knew I was conquered.

Then I came back to life. I suddenly realized that it was mid-day, in the open air between the bald prairie-floor and God's own blue sky, where Olie could stumble on us at any moment—and possibly die with his boots on! Dinky-Dunk was kissing my left eyelid. It was a cup his lips just seemed to fit into. I tried to move. But he held me there. He held me so firmly that it hurt. Yet I couldn't help hugging him. Poor, big, foolish, baby-hearted Dinky-Dunk! And poor, weak, crazy, storm-tossed me! But, oh, God, it's glorious, in some mysterious way, to stir the blood of a strong big man! It's heaven—and I don't quite know why. But I love to see Dinky-Dunk's eyes grow black. Yet it makes me a little afraid of him. I can hear his heart pound, sometimes, quite distinctly. And sometimes there seems something so pathetic about it all—we are such puny little mites of emotion played on by nature for her own immitigable ends! But every woman wants to be loved. Dinky-Dunk asked me why I shut my eyes when he kisses me. I wonder why? Sometimes, too, he says my kisses are wicked, and that he likes 'em wicked. He's a funny mixture. He's got the soul of a Scotch Calvinist tangled up in him somewhere, and after the storm he's very apt to grow pious and a bit preachy. But he has feelings, only he's ashamed of them. I think I'm taking a little of the ice-crust off his emotions. He's a stiff clay that needs to be well stirred up and turned over before it can mellow. And I must be a sandy loam that wastes all its strength in one short harvest. That sounds as though I were getting to be a real farmer's wife with a vast knowledge of soils, doesn't it? At any rate my husband, out of his vast knowledge of me, says I have the swamp-cedar trick of flaring up into sudden and explosive attractiveness. Then, he says, I shower sparks. As I've already told him, I'm a wild woman, and will be hard to tame, for as Victor Hugo somewhere says, we women are only perfected devils!

Wednesday the Eighth

I've cut off my hair, right bang off. When I got up yesterday morning with so much work ahead of me, with so much to do and so little time to do it in, I started doing my hair. I also started thinking about that Frenchman who committed suicide after counting up the number of buttons he had to button and unbutton every morning and evening of every day of every year of his life. I tried to figure up the time I was wasting on that mop of mine. Then the Great Idea occurred to me.

I got the scissors, and in six snips had it off, a big tangled pile of brownish gold, rather bleached out by the sun at the ends. And the moment I saw it there on my dresser, and saw my head in the mirror, I was sorry. I looked like a plucked crow. I could have ditched a freight-train. And I felt positively light-headed. But it was too late for tears. I trimmed off the ragged edges as well as I could, and what didn't get in my eyes got down my neck and itched so terribly that I had to change my clothes. Then I got a nail-punch out of Dinky-Dunk's tool-kit, and heated it over the lamp and gave a little more wave to that two-inch shock of stubble. It didn't look so bad then, and when I tried on Dinky-Dunk's coat in front of the glass I saw that I wouldn't make such a bad-looking boy.

But I waited until noon with my heart in my mouth, to see what Dinky-Dunk would say. What he really *did* say I can't write here, for there was a wicked swear-word mixed up in his ejaculation of startled wonder. Then he saw the tears in my eyes, I suppose, for he came running toward me with his arms out, and hugged me tight, and said I looked cute, and all he'd have to do would be to get used to it. But all dinner time he kept looking at me as though I were a strange woman, and later I saw him standing in front of the dresser, stooping over that tragic pile of tangled yellow-brown snakes. It reminded me of a man stooping over a grave. I slipped away without letting him see me. But this morning I woke him up early and asked him if he still loved his wife. And when he vowed he did, I tried to make him tell me how much. But that stumped him. He compromised by saying he couldn't cheapen his love by defining it in words; it was limitless. I followed him out after breakfast, with a hunger in my heart which bacon and eggs hadn't helped a bit, and told him that if he really loved me he could tell me how much.

He looked right in my eyes, a little pityingly, it seemed to me, and laughed, and grew solemn again. Then he stooped down and picked up a little blade of prairie-grass, and held it up in front of me.

"Have you any idea of how far it is from the Rockies across to the Hudson Bay and from the Line up to the Peace River Valley?"

Of course I hadn't.

"And have you any idea of how many millions of acres of land that is, and how many millions of blades of grass like this there are in each acre?" he soberly demanded.

And again of course I hadn't.

"Well, this one blade of grass is the amount of love I am able to express for you, and all those other blades in all those millions of acres is what love itself is!"

I thought it over, just as solemnly as he had said it. I think I was satisfied. For when my Dinky-Dunk was away off on the prairie, working like a nailer, and I was alone in the shack, I went to his old coat hanging there—the old coat that had some subtle aroma of Dinky-Dunkiness itself about every inch of it—and kissed it on the sleeve.

This afternoon as Paddy and I started for home with a pail of mushrooms I rode face to face with my first coyote. We stood staring at each other. My heart bounced right up into my throat, and for a moment I wondered if I was going to be eaten by a starving timber-wolf, with Dinky-Dunk finding my bones picked as clean as those animal-carcasses we see in an occasional buffalo-wallow. I kept up my end of the stare, wondering whether to advance or retreat, and it wasn't until that coyote turned tail and scooted that my courage came back. Then Paddy and I went after him, like the wind. But we had to give up. And at supper Dinky-Dunk told me coyotes were too cowardly to come near a person, and were quite harmless. He said that even when they showed their teeth, the rest of their face was apologizing for the threat. And before supper was over that coyote, at least I suppose it was the same coyote, was howling at the rising full moon. I went out with Dinky-Dunk's gun, but couldn't get near the brute. Then I came back.

"Sing, you son-of-a-gun, sing!" I called out to him from the shack door. And that shocked my lord and master so much that he scolded me, for the first time in his life. And when I poked his Adam's apple with my finger he got on his dignity. He was tired, poor boy, and I should have remembered it. And when I requested him not to stand there and stare at me in the hieratic rigidity of an Egyptian idol I could see a little flush of anger go over his face. He didn't say anything. But he took one of the lamps and a three-year-old *Pall-Mall Magazine* and shut himself up in the bunk-house.

Then I was sorry.

I tiptoed over to the door, and found it was locked. Then I went and got my mouth-organ and sat meekly down on the doorstep and began to play the *Don't Be Cross* waltz. I dragged it out plaintively, with a *vox humana tremolo* on the coaxing little refrain. Finally I heard a smothered snort, and the door suddenly opened and Dinky-Dunk picked me up, mouth-organ and all. He shook me and said I was a little devil, and I called him a big British brute. But he was laughing and a wee bit ashamed of his temper and was very nice to me all the rest of the evening.

I'm getting, I find, to depend a great deal on Dinky-Dunk, and it makes me afraid, sometimes, for the future. He seems able to slip a hand under my heart and lift it up, exactly as though it were the chin of a wayward child. Yet I resent his power, and keep elbowing for more breathing-space, like a rush-hour passenger in the subway crowd. Sometimes, too, I resent the over-solemn streak in his mental make-up. He abominates ragtime, and I have rather a weakness for it. So once or twice in his dour days I've found an almost Satanic delight in singing *The Humming Coon*. And the knowledge that he'd like to forbid me singing rag seems to give a zest to it. So I go about flashing my saber of independence:

"Ol' Ephr'm Johnson was a deacon of de church in Tennessee, An' of course it was ag'inst de rules t' sing ragtime melodée!"

But I am the one, I notice, who always makes up first. To-night as I was making cocoa before we went to bed I tried to tell my Diddums there was something positively doglike in my devotion to him. He nickered like a pony and said he was the dog in this deal. Then he pulled me over on his knee and said that men get short-tempered when they were tuckered out with worry and hard work, and that probably it would be hard for even two of the seraphim always to get along together in a two-by-four shack, where you couldn't even have, a deadline for the sake of dignity. It was mostly his fault, he knew, but he was going to try to fight against it. And I experienced the unreasonable joy of an unreasonable woman who has succeeded in putting the man she loves with all her heart and soul in the wrong. So I could afford to be humble myself, and make a foolish lot of fuss over him. But I shall always fight for my elbow-room. For there are times when my Dinky-Dunk, for all his bigness and strength, has to be taken sedately in tow, the same as a racing automobile has to be hauled through the city streets by a dinky little low-power hack-car!

Saturday the Tenth

We've had a cold spell, with heavy frosts at night, but the days are still glorious. The overcast days are so few in the West that I've been wondering if the optimism of the Westerners isn't really due to the sunshine they get. Who could be gloomy under such golden skies? Every pore of my body has a throat and is shouting out a *Tarentella Sincera* of its own! But it isn't the weather that has keyed me up this time. It's another wagon-load of supplies which Olie teamed out from Buckhorn yesterday. I've got wall-paper and a new iron bed for the annex, and galvanized wash-tubs and a crock-churn and storm-boots and enough ticking to make ten big pillows, and unbleached linen for two dozen slips—I love a big pillow—and I've been saving up wild-duck feathers for weeks, the downiest feathers you ever sank your ear into, Matilda Anne; and if pillows will do it I'm going to make this house look like a harem! Can you imagine a household with only three pillow-slips, which had to be jerked off in the morning, washed, dried and ironed and put back on their three lonely little pillows before bedtime? Well, there will be no more of that in this shack.

But the important news is that I've got a duck-gun, the duckiest duck-gun you ever saw, and waders, and a coon-skin coat and cap and a big leather school-bag for wearing over my shoulder on Paddy. The coat and cap are like the ones we used to laugh at when we went up to Montreal for the tobogganing, in the days when I was young and foolish and willing to sacrifice comfort on the altar of outward appearances. The coon-skins make me look like a Laplander, but they'll be mighty comfy when the cold weather comes, for Dinky-Dunk says it drops to forty and fifty below, sometimes.

I also got a lot of small stuff I'd written for from the mail-order house, little feminine things a woman simply *has* to have. But the big thing was the duck-gun.

I no longer get heart failure when I hear the whir of a prairie-chicken, but drop my bird before it's out of range. Poor, plump, wounded, warm-bodied little feathery things! Some of them keep on flying after they've been shot clean through the body, going straight on for a couple of hundred feet, or even more, and then dropping like a stone. How hard-hearted we soon get! It used to worry me. Now I gather 'em up as though they were so many chips and toss them into the wagon-box; or into my school-bag, if it's a private expedition of only Paddy and me. And that's the way life treats us, too.

I've been practising on the gophers with my new gun, and with Dinky-Dunk's .22 rifle. A gopher is only a little bigger than a chipmunk, and usually pokes nothing more than his head out of his hole, so when I got thirteen out of fifteen shots I began to feel that I was a sharp-shooter. But don't regard this as wanton cruelty, for the gopher is worse than a rat, and in this country the government agents supply homesteaders with an annual allowance of free strychnine to poison them off.

Sunday the Eleventh

I've made my first butter, be it recorded—but in doing so I managed to splash the ceiling and the walls and my own woolly head, for I didn't have sense enough to tie a wet cloth about the handle of the churn-dasher until the damage had been done. I was too intent on getting my butter to pay attention to details, though it took a disheartening long time and my arms were tired out before I had finished. And when I saw myself spattered from head to foot it reminded me of what you once said about me and my reading, that I had the habit of coming out of a book like a spaniel out of water, scattering ideas as I came. But there are not many new books in my life these days. It is mostly hard work, although I reminded Dinky-Dunk last night that while Omar intimated that love and bread and wine were enough for any wilderness, we mustn't forget that he also included a book of verses underneath the bough! My lord says that by next year we can line our walls with books. But I'm like Moses on Mount Nebo—I can see my promised land, but it seems a terribly long way off. But this, as Dinky-Dunk would say, is not the spirit that built Rome, and has carried me away from my butter, the making of which cold-creamed my face until I looked as though I had snow on my headlight. Yet there is real joy in finding those lovely yellow granules in the bottom of your churn and then working it over and over with a saucer in a cooking-bowl until it is one golden mass. Several times before I'd shaken up sour cream in a sealer, but this was my first real butter-making. I have just discovered, however, that I didn't "wash" it enough, so that all the buttermilk wasn't worked out of my first dairy-product. Dinky-Dunk, like the scholar and gentleman that he is, swore that it was worth its weight in Klondike gold. And next time I'll do better.

Monday the Twelfth

Golden weather again, with a clear sky and soft and balmy air! Just before our mid-day meal Olie arrived with mail for us. We've had letters from home! Instead of cheering me up they made me blue, for they seemed to bring word from another world, a world so far, far away!

I decided to have a half-day in the open, so I strapped on my duck-gun and off I went on Paddy, as soon as dinner was over and the men had gone. We went like the wind, until both Paddy and I were tired of it. Then I found a "soft-water" pond hidden behind a fringe of scrub-willow and poplar. The mid-day sun had warmed it to a tempting temperature. So I hobbled Paddy, peeled off and had a most glorious bath. I had just soaped down with bank-mud (which is an astonishingly good solvent) and had taken a header and was swimming about on my back, blinking up at the blue sky, as happy as a mud-turtle in a mill-pond, when I heard Paddy nicker. That disturbed me a little, but I felt sure there could be nobody within miles of me. However, I swam back to where my clothes were, sunned myself dry, and was just standing up to shake out the ends of this short-cropped hair of mine when I saw a man's head Across the pond, staring through the bushes at me. I don't know how or why it is, but I suddenly saw red. I don't remember picking up the duck-gun, and I don't remember aiming it.

But I banged away, with both barrels, straight at that leering head—or at least it ought to have been a leering head, whatever that may mean! The howl that went up out of the wilderness, the next moment, could have been heard for a mile!

It was Dinky-Dunk, and he said I might have put his eyes out with bird-shot, if he hadn't made the quickest drop of his life. And he also said that he'd seen me, a distinct splash of white against the green of the prairie, three good miles away, and wasn't I ashamed of myself, and what would I have done if he'd been Olie or old man Dixon? But he kissed my shoulder where the gun-stock had bruised it, and helped me dress.

Then we rode off together, four or five miles north, where Dinky-Dunk was sure we could get a bag of duck. Which we did, thirteen altogether, and started for home as the sun got low and the evening air grew chilly. It was a heavenly ride. In the west a little army of thin blue clouds was edged with blazing gold, and up between them spread great fan-like shafts of amber light. Then came a riot of orange yellow and ashes of roses and the palest of gold with little islands of azure in it. Then while the dying radiance seemed to hold everything in a luminous wash of air, the stars came out, one by one, and a soft cool wind swept across the prairie, and the light darkened—and I was glad to have Dinky-Dunk there at my side, or I should have had a little cry, for the twilight prairie always makes me lonesome in a way that could never be put into words.

I tried to explain the feeling to Dinky-Dunk. He said he understood. "I'm a Sour-Dough, Gee-Gee, but it still gets me that way," he solemnly confessed. He said that when he listened to beautiful music he felt the same. And that got me thinking of grand opera, and of that *Romeo and Juliet* night at La Scala, in Milan, when I first met Theobald Gustav. Then I stopped to tell Dinky-Dunk that I'd been hopelessly in love with a tenor at thirteen and had written in my journal: "I shall die and turn to dust still adoring him." Then I told him about my first opera, *Rigoletto*, and hummed "*La Donna E Mobile*," which of course he remembered himself. It took me back to Florence, and to a box at the Pagliano, and me all in dimity and cork-screw curls, weeping deliciously at a lady in white, whose troubles I could not quite understand. Then I got thinking of New York and the Metropolitan, and poor old Morris's lines:

And still with listening soul I hearStrains hushed for many a noisy year:The passionate chords which wake the tear,The low-voiced love-tales dear.... Scarce changed, the same musicians playThe selfsame themes to-day;The silvery swift sonatas ring,The soaring voices sing!

And I could picture the old Metropolitan on a Caruso night. I could see the Golden Horse-Shoe and the geranium-red trimmings and the satiny white backs of the women, and smell that luxurious heavy smell of warm air and hothouse flowers and Paris perfumery and happy human bodies and hear the whisper of silk along the crimson stairways. I could see the lights go down, in a sort of sigh, before the overture began, and the scared-looking blotches of white on the musicians' scores and the other blotches made by their dress-shirt fronts, and the violins going up and down, up and down, as though they were one piece of machinery, and then the heavy curtain stealing up, and the thrill as that new heaven opened up to me, a gawky girl in her first low-cut dinner gown!

I told Dinky-Dunk I'd sat in every corner of that old house, up in the sky-parlor with the Italian barbers, in press-seats in the second gallery with dear old Fanny-Rain-in-the-Face, and in the Westbury's box with the First Lady of the Land and a Spanish Princess with extremely dirty nails. It seemed so far away, another life and another world! And for three hours of "Manon" I'd be willing to hang like a chimpanzee from the Metropolitan's center chandelier. I suddenly realized how much I missed it. I could have sung to the City as poor Charpentier's "Louise" sang to her Paris. And a coyote howled up near the trail, and the prairie got dark, with a pale green rind of light along the northwest, and I knew there would be a heavy frost before morning.

To-night after supper my soul and I sat down and did a bit of bookkeeping. Dinky-Dunk, who'd been watching me out of the corner of his eye, went to the window and said it looked like a storm. And I knew he meant that I was the Medicine Hat it was to come from, for before he'd got up from the table he'd explained to me that matrimony was like motoring because it was really traveling by means of a series of explosions. Then he tried to explain that in a few weeks the fall rush would be over and we'd have more time for getting what we deserved out of life. But I turned on him with sudden fierceness and declared I wasn't going to be merely an animal. I intended to keep my soul alive, that it was every one's duty, no matter where they were, to ennoble their spirit by keeping in touch with the best that has ever been felt and thought.

When I grimly got out my mouth-organ and played the *Pilgrim's Chorus*, as well as I could remember it, Dinky-Dunk sat listening in silent wonder. He kept up the fire, and waited until I got through. Then he reached for the dish-pan and said, quite casually, "I'm going to help you wash up to-night, Gee-Gee!" And so I put away the mouth-organ and washed up. But before I went to bed I got out my little vellum edition of Browning's *The Ring and the Book*, and read at it industriously, doggedly, determinedly, for a solid hour. What it's all about I don't know. Instead of ennobling my spirit it only tired my brain and ended up in making me so mad I flung the book into the wood-box.... Dinky-Dunk has just pinned a piece of paper on my door; it is a sentence from Epictetus. And it says: "Better it is that great souls should live in small habitations than that abject slaves should burrow in great houses!"

Sunday the Eighteenth

I spent an hour to-day trying to shoot a hen-hawk that's been hovering about the shack all afternoon. He's after my chickens, and as new-laid eggs are worth more than Browning to a homesteader, I got out my duck-gun. It gave me a feeling of impending evil, having that huge bird hanging about. It reminded me there was wrong and rapine in the world. I hated the brute. But I hid under one of the wagon-boxes and got him, in the end. I brought him down, a tumbling flurry of wings, like Satan's fall from Heaven. When I ran out to possess myself of his Satanic body he was only wounded, however, and was ready to show fight. Then I saw red again. I clubbed him with the gun-butt, going at him like fury. I was moist with perspiration when I got through with him. He was a monster. I nailed him with his wings out, on the bunk-house wall, and Olie shouted and called Dinky-Dunk when they came back from rounding up the horses, which had got away on the range. Dinky-Dunk solemnly warned me not to run risks, as he might have taken an eye out, or torn my face with his claws. He said he could have stuffed and mounted my hawk, if I hadn't clubbed the poor thing almost to pieces. There's a devil in me somewhere, I told Dinky-Dunk. But he only laughed.

Monday the Nineteenth

To-night Dinky-Dunk and I spent a solid hour trying to decide on a name for the shack. I wanted to call it "Crucknacoola," which is Gaelic for "A Little Hill of Sleep," but Dinky-Dunk brought forward the objection that there was no hill. Then I suggested "Barnavista," since about all we can see from the door are the stables. Then I said "The Builtmore," in a spirit of mockery, and then Dinky-Dunk in a spirit of irony suggested "Casa Grande." And in the end we united on "Casa Grande." It is marvelous how my hair grows. Olie now watches me studiously as I eat. I can see that he is patiently patterning his table deportment after mine. There's nothing that silent rough-mannered man wouldn't do for me. I've got so I never notice his nose, any more than I used to notice Uncle Carlton's receding chin. But I don't think Olie is getting enough to eat. All his mind seems taken up with trying to remember not to drink out of his saucer, as history sayeth George Washington himself once did!

Tuesday the Twentieth

I knew that old hen-hawk meant trouble for me—and the trouble came, all right. I'm afraid I can't tell about it very coherently, but this is how it began: I was alone yesterday afternoon, busy in the shack, when a Mounted Policeman rode up to the door, and, for a moment, nearly frightened the life out of me. I just stood and stared at him, for he was the first really, truly live man, outside Olie and my husband, I'd seen for so long. And he looked very dashing in his scarlet jacket and yellow facings. But I didn't have long to meditate on his color scheme, for he calmly announced that a ranchman named McMein had been murdered by a drunken cowboy in a wage dispute, and the murderer had been seen heading for the Cochrane Ranch. He (the M. P.) inquired if I would object to his searching the buildings.

Would I object? I most assuredly did not, for little chills began to play up and down my spinal column, and I wasn't exactly in love with the idea of having an escaped murderer crawling out of a hay-stack at midnight and cutting my throat. The ranchman McMein had been killed on Saturday, and the cowboy had been kept on the run for two days. As I was being told this I tried to remember where Dinky-Dunk had stowed away his revolver-holster and his hammerless ejector and his Colt repeater. But I made that handsome young man in the scarlet coat come right into the shack and begin his search by looking under the bed, and then going down the cellar.

I stood holding the trap-door and warned him not to break my pickle-jars. Then he came up and stood squinting thoughtfully out through the doorway.

"Have you got a gun?" he suddenly asked me.

I showed him my duck-gun with its silver mountings, and he smiled a little.

"Haven't you a rifle?" he demanded.

I explained that my husband had, and he still stood squinting out through the doorway as I poked about the shack-corners and found Dinky-Dunk's repeater. He was a very authoritative and self-assured young man. He took the rifle from me, examined the magazine and made sure it was loaded. Then he handed it back.

"I've got to search those buildings and stacks," he told me. "And I can only be in one place at once. If you see a man break from under cover anywhere, when I'm inside, *be so good as to shoot him*!"

He started off without another word, with his big army revolver in his hand. My teeth began to do a little fox-trot all by themselves.

"Wait! Stop!" I shouted after him. "Don't go away!"

He stopped and asked me what was wrong. "I—I don't want to shoot a man! I don't want to shoot *any* man!" I tried to explain to him.

"You probably won't have to," was his cool response. "But it's better to do that than have him shoot *you*, isn't it?"

Whereupon Mr. Red-Coat made straight for the hay-stacks, and I stood in the doorway, with Dinky-Dunk's rifle in my hands and my knees shaking a little.

I watched him as he beat about the hay-stacks. Then I got tired of holding the heavy weapon and leaned it against the shack-wall. I watched the red coat go in through the stable door, and felt vaguely dismayed at the thought that its wearer was now quite out of sight.

Then my heart stopped beating. For out of a pile of straw which Olie had dumped not a hundred feet away from the house, to line a pit for our winter vegetables, a man suddenly erupted. He seemed to come up out of the very earth, like a mushroom.

He was the most repulsive-looking man I ever had the pleasure of casting eyes on. His clothes were ragged and torn and stained with mud. His face was covered with stubble and his cheeks were hollow, and his skin was just about the color of a new saddle.

I could see the whites of his eyes as he ran for the shack, looking over his shoulder toward the stable door as he came. He had a revolver in his hand. I noticed that, but it didn't seem to trouble me much. I suppose I'd already been frightened as much as mortal flesh could be frightened. In fact, I was thinking quite clearly what to do, and didn't hesitate for a moment.

"Put that silly thing down," I told him, as he ran up to me with his head lowered and that indescribably desperate look in his big frightened eyes. "If you're not a fool I can get you hidden," I told him. It reassured me to see that his knees were shaking much more than mine, as he stood there in the center of the shack! I stooped over the trap-door and lifted it up. "Get down there quick! He's searched that cellar and won't go through it again. Stay there until I say he's gone!"

He slipped over to the trap-door and went slowly down the steps, with his eyes narrowed and his revolver held up in front of him, as though he still half expected to find some one there to confront him with a blunderbuss. Then I promptly shut the trap-door. But there was no way of locking it.

I had my murderer there, trapped, but the question was to keep him there. Your little Chaddie didn't give up many precious moments to reverie. I tiptoed into the bedroom and lifted the mattress, bedding and all, off the bedstead. I tugged it out and put it silently down over the trap-door. Then, without making a sound, I turned the table over on it. But he could still lift that table, I knew, even with me sitting on top of it. So I started to pile things on the overturned table, until it looked like a moving-van ready for a May-Day migration. Then I sat on top of that pile of household goods, reached for Dinky-Dunk's repeater, and deliberately fired a shot up through the open door.

I sat there, studying my pile, feeling sure a revolver bullet couldn't possibly come up through all that stuff. But before I had much time to think about this my corporal of the R. N. W. M. P. (which means, Matilda Anne, the Royal North-West Mounted Police) came through the door on the run. He looked relieved when he saw me triumphantly astride that overturned table loaded up with about all my household junk.

"I've got him for you," I calmly announced.

"You've got what?" he said, apparently thinking I'd gone mad.

"I've got your man for you," I repeated. "He's down there in my cellar." And in one minute I'd explained just what had happened. There was no parley, no deliberation, no hesitation.

"Hadn't you better go outside," he suggested as he started piling the things off the trap-door.

"You're not going down there?" I demanded.

"Why not?" he asked.

"But he's got a revolver," I cried out, "and he's sure to shoot!"

"That's why I think it might be better for you to step outside for a moment or two," was my soldier boy's casual answer.

I walked over and got Dinky-Dunk's repeater. Then I crossed to the far side of the shack, with the rifle in my hands.

"I'm going to stay," I announced.

"All right," was the officer's unconcerned answer as he tossed the mattress to one side and with one quick pull threw up the trap-door.

A shot rang out, from below, as the door swung back against the wall. But it was not repeated, for the man in the red coat jumped bodily, heels first, into that black hole. He didn't seem to count on the risk, or on what might be ahead of him. He just jumped, spurs down, on that other man with the revolver in his hand. I could hear little grunts, and wheezes, and a thud or two against the cellar steps. Then there was silence, except for one double "click-click" which I couldn't understand.

Oh, Matilda Anne, how I watched that cellar opening! And I saw a back with a red coat on it slowly rise out of the hole. He, the man who owned the back of course, was dragging the other man bodily up the narrow little stairs. There was a pair of handcuffs already on his wrists and he seemed dazed and helpless, for that slim-looking soldier boy had pummeled him unmercifully, knocking out his two front teeth, one of which I found on the doorstep when I was sweeping up.

"I'm sorry, but I'll have to take one of your horses for a day or two," was all my R. N. W. M. P. hero condescended to say to me as he poked an arm through his prisoner's and helped him out through the door.

"What—what will they do with him?" I called out after the corporal.

"Hang him, of course," was the curt answer.

Then I sat down to think things over, and, like an old maid with the vapors, decided I wouldn't be any the worse for a cup of good strong tea. And by the time I'd had my tea, and straightened things up, and incidentally discovered that no less than five of my cans of mushrooms had been broken to bits below-stairs, I heard the rumble of the wagon and knew that Olie and Dinky-Dunk were back. And I drew a long breath of relief, for with all their drawbacks, men are not a bad thing to have about, now and then!

Thursday the Twenty-second

It was early Tuesday morning that Dinky-Dunk firmly announced that he and I were going off on a three-day shooting-trip. I hadn't slept well, the night before, for my nerves were still rather upset, and Dinky-Dunk said I needed a picnic. So we got guns and cartridges and blankets and slickers and cooking things, and stowed them away in the wagon-box. Then we made a list of the provisions we'd need, and while Dinky-Dunk bagged up some oats for the team I was busy packing the grub-box. And I packed it cram full, and took along the old tin bread-box, as well, with pancake flour and dried fruit and an extra piece of bacon—and *bacon* it is now called in this shack, for I have positively forbidden Dinky-Dunk ever to speak of it as "sowbelly" or even as a "slice of grunt" again.

Then off we started across the prairie, after duly instructing Olie as to feeding the chickens and taking care of the cream and finishing up the pit for the winter vegetables. Still once again Olie thought we were both a little mad, I believe, for we had no more idea where we were going than the man in the moon.

But there was something glorious in the thought of gipsying across the autumn prairie like that, without a thought or worry as to where we must stop or what trail we must take. It made every day's movement a great adventure. And the weather was divine.

We slept at night under the wagon-box, with a tarpaulin along one side to keep out the wind, and a fire flickering in our faces on the other side, and the horses tethered out, and the stars wheeling overhead, and the peace of God in our hearts. How good every meal tasted! And how that keen sharp air made snuggling down under a couple of Hudson Bay five-point blankets a luxury to be spoken of only in the most reverent of whispers! And there was a time, as you already know, when I used to take bromide and sometimes even sulphonal to make me sleep! But here it is so different! To get leg-weary in the open air, tramping about the sedgy slough-sides after mallard and canvas-back, to smell coffee and bacon and frying grouse in the cool of the evening, across a thin veil of camp-fire smoke, to see the tired world turn over on its shoulder and go to sleep—it's all a sort of monumental lullaby.

The prairie wind seems to seek you out, and make a bet with the Great Dipper that he'll have you off in forty winks, and the orchestra of the spheres whispers through its million strings and sings your soul to rest. For I tell you here and now, Matilda Anne, I, poor, puny, good-for-nothing, insignificant I, have heard that music of the spheres as clearly as you ever heard *Funiculi-Funicula* on that little Naples steamer that used to take you to Capri. And when I'd crawl out from under that old wagon-box, like a gopher out of his hole, in the first delicate rosiness of dawn, I'd feel unutterably grateful to be alive, to hear the cantatas of health singing deep in my soul, to know that whatever life may do to me, I'd snatched my share of happiness from the pantry of the gods! And the endless change of color, from the tawny fox-glove on the lighter land, the pale yellow of a lion's skin in the slanting autumn sun, to the quavering, shimmering glories of the Northern Lights that dance in the north, that fling out their banners of ruby and gold and green, and tremble and merge and pulse until I feel that I can hear the clash of invisible cymbals. I wonder if you can understand my feeling when I pulled the hat-pin out of my old gray Stetson yesterday, uncovered my head, and looked straight up into the blue firmament above me. Then I said, "Thank you, God, for such a beautiful day!"

Dinky-Dunk promptly said that I was blasphemous—he's so strict and solemn! But as I stared up into the depths of that intense opaline light, so clear, so pure, I realized how air, just air and nothing else, could leave a scatter-brained lady like me half-seas over. Only it's a champagne that never leaves you with a headache the next day!

Saturday the Twenty-fourth

Dinky-Dunk, who seems intent on keeping my mind occupied, brought me home a bundle of old magazines last night. They were so frayed and thumbed-over that some of the pages reminded me of well-worn banknotes. I've been reading some of the stories, and they all seem silly. Everybody appears to be in love with somebody else's wife. Then the people are all divided so strictly into two classes, the good and the bad! As for the other man's wife, prairie-life would soon knock that nonsense out of people. There isn't much room for the Triangle in a two-by-four shack. Life's so normal and natural and big out here that a Pierre Loti would be kicked into a sheep-dip before he could use up his first box of face-rouge! You want your own wife, and want her so bad you're satisfied. Not that Dinky-Dunk and I are so goody-goody! We're just healthy and human, that's all, and we'd never do for fiction. After meals we push away the dishes and sit side by side, with our arms across each other's shoulders, full of the joy of life, satisfied, happy, healthy-minded, now and then a little Rabelaisian in our talk, meandering innocent-eyed through those earthier intimacies which most married people seem to face without shame, so long as the facing is done in secret. We don't seem ashamed of that terribly human streak in us. And neither of us is bad, at heart. But I know we're not like those magazine characters, who all seem to have Florida-water instead of red blood in their veins, and are so far, far away from life.

Yet even that dip into politely erotic fiction seemed to canalize my poor little grass-grown mind into activity, and Diddums and I sat up until the wee sma' hours discoursing on life and letters. He started me off by somewhat pensively remarking that all women seem to want to be intellectual and have a *salon*.

"No, Dinky-Dunk, I don't want a *salon*," I promptly announced. "I never did want one, for I don't believe they were as exciting as we imagine. And I hate literary people almost as much as I hate actors. I always felt they were like stage-scenery, not made for close inspection. For after five winters in New York and a couple in London you can't help bumping into the Bohemian type, not to mention an occasional collision with 'em up and down the Continent. When they're female they always seem to wear the wrong kind of corsets. And when they're male they watch themselves in the mirrors, or talk so much about themselves that you haven't a chance to talk about *yourself*—which is really the completest definition of a bore, isn't it? I'd much rather know them through their books than through those awful Sunday evening *soirees* where poor old leonine M—— used to perspire reading those Socialist poems of his to the adoring ladies, and Sanguinary John used to wear the same flannel shirt that shielded him from the Polar blasts up in Alaska—open at the throat, and all that sort of thing, just like a movie-actor cowboy, only John had grown a little stout and he kept spoiling the Strong-Man picture by so everlastingly posing at one end of the grand-piano! You know the way they do it, one pensive elbow on the piano-end and the delicately drooping palm holding up the weary brains, the same as you prop up a King-orange bough when it gets too heavy with fruit! And then he had a lovely bang and a voice like a maiden-lady from Maine. And take it from me, O lord and master, that man devoured all his raw beef and blood on his typewriter-ribbon. I dubbed him the King of the Eye-Socket school, and instead of getting angry he actually thanked me for it. That was the sort of advertising he was after."

Dinky-Dunk grinned a little as I rattled on. Then he grew serious again. "Why is it," he asked, "a writer in Westminster Abbey is always a genius, but a writer in the next room is rather a joke?"

I tried to explain it for him. "Because writers are like Indians. The only good ones are the dead ones. And it's the same with those siren affinities of history. Annie Laurie lived to be eighty, though the ballad doesn't say so. And Lady Hamilton died poor and ugly and went around with red herrings in her pocket. And Cleopatra was really a redheaded old political schemer, and Paris got tired of Helen of Troy. Which means that history, like literature, is only *Le mensonge convenu*!"

This made Dinky-Dunk sit up and stare at me. "Look here, Gee-Gee, I don't mind a bit of book-learning, but I hate to see you tear the whole tree of knowledge up by the roots and knock me down with it! And it was *salons* we were talking about, and not the wicked ladies of the past!"

"Well, the only *salon* I ever saw in America had the commercial air of a millinery opening where tea happened to be served," I promptly declared. "And the only American woman I ever knew who wanted to have a *salon* was a girl we used to call Asafetida Anne. And if I explained why you'd make a much worse face than that, my Diddums. But she had a weakness for black furs and never used to wash her neck. So the Plimpton Mark was always there!"

"Don't get bitter, Gee-Gee," announced Dinky-Dunk as he proceeded to light his pipe. And I could afford to laugh at his solemnity.

"I'm not bitter, Honey Chile; I'm only glad I got away from all that Bohemian rubbish. You may call me a rattle-box, and accuse me of being temperamental now and then—which I'm not—but the one thing in life which I love is *sanity*. And that, Dinky-Dunk, is why I love you, even though you are only a big sunburnt farmer fighting and planning and grinding away for a home for an empty-headed wife who's going to fail at everything but making you love her!"

Then followed a few moments when I wasn't able to talk,

... The sequel's scarce essential—Nay, more than this, I hold it stillProfoundly confidential!

Then as we sat there side by side I got thinking of the past and of the Bohemians before whom I had once burned incense. And remembering a certain visit to Box Hill with Lady Agatha's mother, years and years ago, I had to revise my verdict on authors, for one of the warmest memories in all my life is that of dear old Meredith in his wheelchair, with his bearded face still flooded with its kindly inner light and his spirit still mellow with its unquenchable love of life. And once as a child, I went on to tell Dinky-Dunk, I had met Stevenson. It was at Mentone, and I can still remember him leaning over and taking my hand. His own hand was cold and lean, like a claw, and with the quick instinct of childhood I realized, too, that he was *condescending* as he spoke to me, for all the laugh that showed the white teeth under his drooping black mustache. Wrong as it seemed, I didn't like him any more than I afterward liked the Sargent portrait of him, which was really an echo of my own first impression, though often and often I've tried to blot out that first unfair estimate of a real man of genius. There's so much in the *Child's Garden of Verse* that I love; there's so much in the man's life that demands admiration, that it seems wrong not to capitulate to his charm. But when one's own family are one's biographers it's hard to be kept human. "Yet there's one thing, Dinky-Dunk, that I do respect him for," I went on. "He had seen the loveliest parts of this world, and, when he had to, he could light-heartedly give it all up and rough it in this American West of ours, even as you and I!" Whereupon Dinky-Dunk argued that we ought to forgive an invalid his stridulous preaching about bravery and manliness and his over-emphasis of fortitude, since it was plainly based on an effort to react against a constitutional weakness for which he himself couldn't be blamed.

And I confessed that I could forgive him more easily than I could Sanguinary John with his literary Diabolism and that ostentatious stone-age blugginess with which he loved to give the ladies goose-flesh, pretending he was a bull in a china-shop when he's really only a white mouse in an ink-pot! And after Dinky-Dunk had knocked out his pipe and wound up his watch he looked over at me with his slow Scotch-Canadian smile. "For a couple of hay-seeds who have been harpooning the *salon* idea," he solemnly announced, "I call this quite a literary evening!" But what's the use of having an idea or two in your head if you can't air 'em now and then?

Tuesday the Twenty-seventh

To-day I stumbled on the surprise of my life! It was A Man! I took Paddy and cantered over to the old Titchborne Ranch and was prowling around the corral, hoping I might find a few belated mushrooms. But nary a one was there. So I whistled on my four fingers for Paddy (I've been teaching him to come at that call) and happened to glance in the direction of the abandoned shack. Then I saw the door open, and *out walked a man.*

He was a young man, in puttees and knickers and Norfolk jacket, and he was smoking a cigarette. He stared at me as though I were the Missing Link. Then he said "Hello!" rather inadequately, it seemed to me.

I answered back "Hello," and wondered whether to take to my heels or not. But my courage got its second wind, and I stayed. Then we shook hands, very formally, and explained who we were. And I discovered that his name was Percival Benson Woodhouse (and the Lord forgive me if they ever call him Percy for short!) and that his aunt is the Countess of D—— and that he knows a number of people you and Lady Agatha have often spoken of. He's got a Japanese servant called Kino, or perhaps it's spelt Keeno, I don't know which, who's housekeeper, laundress, *valet*, gardener, groom and *chef*, all in one,—so, at least Percival Benson confessed to me. He also confessed that he'd bought the Titchborne Ranch, from photographs, from "one of those land chaps" in London. He wanted to rough it a bit, and they told him there would be jolly good game shooting. So he even brought along an elephant-gun, which his cousin had used in India. The photographs which the "land chap" had showed him turned out to be pictures of the Selkirks. And, taking it all in all, he fancied that he'd been jolly well bunked. But Percival seemed to accept it with the stoicism of the well-born Britisher. He'd have a try at the place, although there was no game.

"But there *is* game," I told him, "slathers of it, oodles of it!"

He mildly inquired where and what? I told him: Wild duck, prairie-chicken, wild geese, jack-rabbits, now and then a fox, and loads of coyotes. He explained, then, that he meant big game—and how grandly those two words, "big game," do roll off the English tongue! He has a sister in the Bahamas, who may join him next summer if he should decide to stick it out. He considered that it would be a bit rough for a girl, during the winter season up here.

Yet before I go any further I must describe Percival Benson Woodhouse to you, for he's not only "our sort," but a type as well.

In the first place, he's a Magdalen College man, the sort we've seen going up and down the High many and many a time. He's rather gaunt and rather tall, and he stoops a little. "At home" they call it the "Oxford stoop," if I'm not greatly mistaken. His hands are thin and long and bony. His eyes are nice, and he looks very good form. I mean he's the sort of man you'd never take for the "outsider" or "rotter." He's the sort who seem to have the royal privilege of doing even doubtfully polite things and yet doing them in such a way as to make them seem quite proper. I don't know whether I make that clear or not, but one thing is clear, and this is that our Percival Benson is an aristocrat. You see it in his over-sensitive, over-refined, almost womanishly delicate face, with those idealizing and quite unpractical eyes of his. You see it in the thin, high-arched, bony nose (almost as fine a beak as the one belonging to His Grace, the Duke of M——!) and you see it in the sad and somewhat elongated face, as though he had pored over big books too much, a sort of air of pathos and aloofness from things. His mouth strikes you as being rather meager, until he smiles, which is quite often, for, glory be, he has a good sense of humor. But besides that he has a neatness, a coolness, an impersonal sort of ease, which would make you think that he might have stepped out of one of Henry James's earlier novels of about the time of the *Portrait of a Lady*. And I like him. I knew that at once. He's *effete* and old-worldish and probably useless, out here, but he stands for something I've been missing, and I'll be greatly mistaken if Percival Benson and Chaddie McKail are not pretty good friends before the winter's over! He's asked if he might be permitted to call, and he's coming for dinner tomorrow night, and I do hope Dinky-Dunk is nice to him—if we're to be neighbors. But Dinky-Dunk says Westerners don't ask to be permitted to call. They just stick their cayuse into the corral and walk in, the same as an Indian does. And Dinky-Dunk says that if he comes in evening dress he'll shoot him, sure pop!

Thursday the Twenty-ninth

Percy (how I hate that name!) was here for dinner last night, and all things considered, we didn't fare so badly. We had tomato bisque and scalloped potatoes and prairie-chicken (they need to be well basted) and hot biscuits and stewed dried peaches with cream. Then we had coffee and the men smoked their pipes. We talked until a quarter to one in the morning, and my poor Dinky-Dunk, who has been working so hard and seeing nobody, really enjoyed that visit and really likes Percival Benson.

Percy got talking about Oxford, and you could see that he loved the old town and that he felt more at home on the Isis than on the prairie. He said he once heard Freeman tell a story about Goldwin Smith, who used to be Regius Professor of History at the University. G. S. seemed astonished that F. couldn't tell him, at some *viva voce* exam, whatever that may mean, the cause of King John's death. Then G. S. explained that poor John died of too much peaches and fresh ale, "which would give a man considerable belly-ache," the Regius Professor of History solemnly announced to Freeman.

Percy said his lungs rather troubled him in England, and he has spent over a year in Florence and Rome and can talk pictures like a Grant Allen guide-book. And he's sat through many an opera at La Scala, but considered the Canadian coyote a much better vocalist than most of the minor Italian tenors. And he knows Capri and Taormina and says he'd like to grow old and die in Sicily. He got pneumonia at Messina, and nearly died young there and after five months in Switzerland a specialist told him to try Canada.

I've noticed that one of the delusions of Americans is that an Englishman is silent. Now, my personal conviction is that Englishmen are the greatest talkers in the world, and I have Percy to back me up in it. In fact, we sat about talking so long that Percy asked if he couldn't stay all night, as he was a poor rider and wasn't sure of the trails as yet. So we made a shake-down for him in the living-room. And when Dinky-Dunk came to bed he confided to me that Percy was calmly reading and smoking himself to sleep, out of my sadly scorned copy of *The Ring and the Book*, with the lamp on the floor, on one side of him, and a saucer on the other, for an ash-tray. But he was up and out this morning, before either of us was stirring, coming back to Casa Grande, however, when he saw the smoke at the chimney-top. His thin cheeks were quite pink and he apologetically explained that he'd been trying for an hour and a half to catch his cayuse. Olie had come to his rescue. But our thin-shouldered Oxford exile said that he had never seen such a glorious sunrise, and that the ozone had made him a bit tipsy. Speaking of thin-shouldered specimens, Matilda Anne, I was once a thirty-six; *now I am a perfect forty-two.*

Friday the Fifth

The weather has been bad all this week, but I've had a great deal of sewing to do, and for two days Dinky-Dunk stayed in and helped me fix up the shack. I made more book-shelves out of more old biscuit-boxes and my lord made a gun-rack for our fire-arms. Percival Benson rode over once, through the storm, and it took us half an hour to thaw him out. But he brought some books, and says he has four cases, altogether, and that we're welcome to all we wish. He stayed until noon the next day, this time sleeping in the annex, which Dinky-Dunk and I have papered, so that it looks quite presentable. But as yet there is no way of heating it. Our new neighbor, I imagine, is very lonesome.

Sunday the Seventh

The weather has cleared: there's a chinook arch in the sky, and a sort of St. Martin's-Summer haze on all the prairie. But there's news to-day. Kino, our new neighbor's Jap, has decamped with a good deal of money and about all of Percival Benson's valuables. The poor boy is almost helpless, but he's not a quitter. He said he chopped his first kindling to-day, though he had to stand in a wash-tub, while he did it, to keep from cutting his feet. Dinky-Dunk's birthday is only three weeks off, and I'm making plans for a celebration.

Tuesday the Ninth

The days slip by, and scarcely leave me time to write. Dinky-Dunk is a sort of pendulum, swinging out to work, back to eat, and then out, and then back again. Olie is teaming in lumber and galvanized iron for a new building of some sort. My lord, in the evenings, sits with paper and pencil, figuring out measurements and making plans. I sit on the other side of the table, as a rule, sewing. Sometimes I go around to his side of the table, and make him put his plans away for a few minutes. We are very happy. But where the days fly to I scarcely know. We are always looking toward the future, talking about the future, "conceiting" for the future, as the Irish say. Next summer is to be our banner year. Dinky-Dunk is going to risk everything on wheat. He's like a general plotting out a future plan of campaign—for when the work comes, he says, it will come in a rush. Help will be hard to get, so he'll sell his British Columbia timber rights and buy a forty-horse-power gasoline tractor. He will at least if gasoline gets cheaper, for with "gas" still at twenty-six cents a gallon horse-power is cheapest. But during the breaking season in April and May, one of these engines can haul eight gang-plows behind it. In twenty-four hours it will be able to turn over thirty-five acres of prairie soil—and the ordinary man and team counts two acres of plowing a decent day's work.

To-night I asked Dinky-Dunk why he risked everything on wheat and warned him that we might have to revise the old Kansas trekker's slogan to—

"In wheat we trusted,In wheat we busted!

Dinky-Dunk explained that to keep on raising only wheat would be bad for the land, and even now meant taking a chance, but situated as he was it brought in the quickest money. And he wanted money in a hurry, for he had a nest to feather for a lady wild-bird that he'd captured—which meant me. Later on he intends to go in for flax—for fiber and not for seed—and as our land should produce two tons of the finest flax-straw to the acre and as the Belgian and Irish product is now worth over four hundred dollars a ton, he told me to sit down and figure out what four hundred acres would produce, with even a two-third crop.

The Canadian farmer of the West, he went on to explain, mostly grew flax for the seed alone, burning up over a million tons of straw every year, just to get it out of the way, the same as he does with his wheat-straw. But all that will soon be changed. Only last week Dinky-Dunk wrote to the Department of Agriculture for information about *courtai* fiber—that's the kind used for point-lace and is worth a dollar a pound—for my lord feels convinced his soil and climatic conditions are especially suited for certain of the finer varieties. He even admitted that flax would be better on his land at the present time, as it would release certain of the natural fertilizers which sometimes leave the virgin soil too rich for wheat. But what most impressed me about Dinky-Dunk's talk was his absolute and unshaken faith in this West of ours, once it wakes up to its opportunities. It's a stored-up granary of wealth, he declares, and all we've done so far is to nibble along the leaks in the floor-cracks!

Saturday the Twenty-first

To-day is Dinky-Dunk's birthday. He's always thought, of course, that I'm a pauper, and never dreamed of my poor little residuary nest-egg. I'd ordered a box of Okanagan Valley apples, and a gramophone and a dozen opera records, and a brier-wood pipe and two pounds of English "Honey-Dew," and a smoking-jacket, and some new ties and socks and shirts, and a brand new Stetson, for Dinky-Dunk's old hat is almost a rag-bag. And I ordered half a dozen of the newer novels and a set of Herbert Spencer which I heard him say he wanted, and a sepia print of the *Mona Lisa* (which my lord says I look like when I'm planning trouble) and a felt mattress and a set of bed-springs (so good-by, old sway-backed friend whose humps have bruised me in body and spirit this many a night!) and a dozen big oranges and three dozen little candles for the birthday cake. And then I was cleaned out—every blessed cent gone! But Percy (we have, you see, been unable to escape that name) ordered a box of cigars and a pair of quilted house-slippers, so it was a pretty formidable array.

I, accordingly, had Olie secretly team this array all the way from Buckhorn to Percy's house, where it was duly ambushed and entrenched, to await the fatal day. As luck would have it, or seemed to have it, Dinky-Dunk had to hit the trail for overnight, to see about the registration of his transfers for his new half-section, at the town of H———. So as soon as Dinky-Dunk was out of sight I hurried through my work and had Tumble-Weed and Bronk headed for the old Titchborne Ranch.

There I arrived about mid-afternoon, and what a time we had, getting those things unpacked, and looking them over, and planning and talking! But the whole thing was spoilt.

We forgot to tie the horses. So while we were having tea Bronk and Tumble-Weed hit the trail, on their own hook. They made for home, harness and all, but of course I never knew this at the time. We looked and looked, came back for supper, and then started out again. We searched until it got dark. My feet were like lead, and I couldn't have walked another mile. I was so stiff and tired I simply had to give up. Percy worried, of course, for we had no way of sending word to Dinky-Dunk. Then we sat down and talked over possibilities, like a couple of castaways on a Robinson Crusoe island. Percy offered to bunk in the stable, and let me have the shack. But I wouldn't hear of that. In the first place, I felt pretty sure Percy was what they call a "lunger" out here, and I didn't relish the idea of sleeping in a tuberculous bed. I asked for a blanket and told him that I was going to sleep out under the wagon, as I'd often done with Dinky-Dunk. Percy finally consented, but this worried him too. He even brought out his "big-game" gun, so I'd have protection, and felt the grass to see if it was damp, and declared he couldn't sleep on a mattress when he knew I was out on the hard ground. I told him that I loved it, and to go to bed, for I wanted to get out of some of my armor-plate. He went, reluctantly.

It was a beautiful night, and not so cold, with scarcely a breath of wind stirring. I lay looking out through the wheel-spokes at the Milky Way, and was just dropping off when Percy came out still again. He was in a quilted dressing-gown and had a blanket over his shoulders. It made him look for all the world like Father Time. He wanted to know if I was all right, and had brought me out a pillow—which I didn't use. Then he sat down on the prairie-floor, near the wagon, and smoked and talked. He pointed out some of the constellations to me, and said the only time he'd ever seen the stars bigger was one still night on the Indian Ocean, when he was on his way back from Singapore. He would never forget that night, he said, the stars were so wonderful, so big, so close, so soft and luminous. But the northern stars were different. They were without the orange tone that belongs to the South. They seemed remoter and more awe-inspiring, and there was always a green tone to their whiteness.

Then we got talking about "furrin parts" and Percy asked me if I'd ever seen Naples at night from San Martino, and I asked him if he'd ever seen Broadway at night from the top of the Times Building. Then he asked me if I'd ever watched Paris from Montmartre, or seen the Temple of Neptune at Pæstum bathed in Lucanian moonlight—which I very promptly told him I had, for it was on the ride home from Pæstum that a certain person had proposed to me. We talked about temples and Greek Gods and the age of the world and Indian legends until I got downright sleepy. Then Percy threw away his last cigarette and got up. He said "Good night;" I said "Good night;" and he went into the shack. He said he'd leave the door open, in case I called. There were just the two of us, between earth and sky, that night, and not another soul within a radius of seven miles of any side of us. He was very glad to have some one to talk to. He's probably a year or two older than I am, but I am quite motherly with him. And he is shockingly incompetent, as a homesteader, from the look of his shack. But he's a gentleman, almost too "Gentle," I sometimes feel, a Laodicean, mentally over-refined until it leaves him unable to cope with real life. He's one of those men made for being a "spectator," and not an actor, in life. And there's something so absurd about his being where he is that I feel sorry for him.

I slept like a log. Once I fell asleep, I forgot about the hard ground, and the smell of the horse-blankets, and the fact that I'd lost my poor Dinky-

Dunk's team. When I woke up it was the first gray of dawn. Two men were standing side by side, looking at me under the wagon. One was Percy, and the other was Dinky-Dunk himself.

He'd got home by three o'clock in the morning, by hurrying, for he was nervous about me being alone. But he found the house empty, the team standing beside the corral, and me missing. Naturally, it wasn't a very happy situation. Poor Dinky-Dunk hit the trail at once, and had been riding all night looking for his lost wife. Then he made for Percy's, woke him up, and discovered her placidly snoring under a wagon-box. He didn't even smile at this. He was very tired and very silent. I thought, for a moment, that I saw distrust on Dinky-Dunk's face, for the first time. But he has said nothing. I hated to see him go out to work, when we got home, but he refused to take a nap at noon, as I wanted him to. So to-night, when he came in for his supper, I had the birthday cake duly decked and the presents all out.

But his enthusiasm was forced, and all during the meal he showed a tendency to be absent-minded. I had no explanations to make, so I made none. But I noticed that he put on his old slippers. I thought he had done it deliberately.

"You don't seem to mellow with age," I announced, with my eyebrows up. He flushed at that, quite plainly. Then he reached over and took hold of my hand. But he did it only with an effort, and after some tremendous inward struggle which was not altogether flattering to me.

"Please take your hand away so I can reach the dish-towel," I told him. And the hand went away like a shot. After I'd finished my work I got out my George Meredith and read *Modern Love*. Dinky-Dunk did not come to bed until late. I was awake when he came, but I didn't let him know it.

Sunday the Twenty-ninth

I haven't felt much like writing this last week. I scarcely know why. I think it's because Dinky-Dunk is on his dignity. He's getting thin, by the way. His cheek-bones show and his Adam's apple sticks out. He's worried about his land payments, and I tell him he'd be happier with a half-section. But Dinky-Dunk wants wealth. And I can't help him much. I'm afraid I'm an encumbrance. And the stars make me lonely, and the prairie wind sometimes gives me the willies! And winter is coming.

I'm afraid I'm out of my setting, as badly out of it as Percival Benson is. It wouldn't be so bad, I suppose, if I'd never seen such lovely corners of the world, before coming out here to be a dot on the wilderness. If I'd never had that heavenly summer at Fiesole, and those months with you at Corfu, and that winter in Rome with poor dear dead Katrinka! Sometimes I think of the nights we used to look out over Paris, from the roof above 'Tite Daneau's studio. And sometimes I think of the Pincio, with the band playing, and the carriages flashing, and the officers in uniform, and the milky white statues among the trees, and the golden mists of the late afternoon over the Immortal City. And I tell myself that it was all a dream. And then I feel that *I* am all a dream, and the prairie is a dream, and Paddy and Olie and Dinky-Dunk and all this new life is nothing more than a dream. Oh, Matilda Anne, I've been homesick this week, so unhappy and homesick for something—for something, and I don't even know what it is!

Monday the Seventh

Glory be! Winter's here with a double-edged saber wind out of the north and snow on the ground. It gives a zip to things. It makes our snug little shack seem as cozy as a ship's cabin. And I've got a jumper-sleigh, and with my coon-skin coat and gauntlets and wedge-cap I can be as warm as toast in any wind. And there's so much to do. And I'm not going to be a piker. This is the land where folks make good or go loco. You've only got yourself to depend on, and yourself to blame, if things go wrong. And I'm going to make them go right. There's no use wailing out here in the West. A line or two of Laurence Hope's has been running all day through my head:

"These are my people, and this my land;I hear the pulse of her secret soul.This is the life that I understand,Savage and simple, and sane and whole."

Friday the Eleventh

Dinky-dunk came home with an Indian girl to-day, a young half-breed about sixteen years old. She's to be both companion and parlor-maid, for Dinky-Dunk has to hurry off to British Columbia, to try to sell his timber-rights there to meet his land payments. He's off to-morrow. It makes me feel wretched, but I'm consuming my own smoke, for I don't want him to think me an encumbrance. My Indian girl speaks a little English. She also eats sugar by the handful, whenever she can steal it. I asked her what her name was and she told me "Queenie MacKenzie." That name almost took my breath away. How that untutored Northwest aborigine ever took unto herself this Broadway chorus-girl name, Heaven only knows! But I have my suspicions of Queenie. She has certain exploratory movements which convince me she is verminous. She sleeps in the annex, I'm happy to say.

At dinner to-night when I was teaching Dinky-Dunk how to make a rabbit out of his table-napkin and a sea-sick passenger out of the last of his oranges, he explained that he might not get back in time for Christmas, and asked if I'd mind. I knew his trip was important, so I kept a stiff upper lip and said of course I wouldn't mind. But the thought of a Christmas alone chilled my heart. I tried to be jolly, and gave my repertory on the mouth-organ, which promptly stopped all activities on the part of the round-eyed Queenie MacKenzie. But all that foolery was as forced as the frivolity of the French Revolution Conciergerie where the merry diners couldn't quite forget they were going to lose their heads in the morning!

Sunday the Thirteenth

Not only is Duncan gone, but Queenie has also quite unceremoniously taken her departure. It arose from the fact that I requested her to take a bath. The only disappointed member of the family is poor old Olie, who was actually making sheep's eyes at that verminous little baggage. Imagination falters at what he might have done with a dollar's worth of brown sugar. When Queenie went, I find, my mouth-organ went with her. I'd like to ling chih that Indian girl!

Wednesday the Sixteenth

It was a sparkling clear day to-day, with no wind, so I rode over to the old Titchborne Ranch with my little jumper-sleigh. There I found Percival Benson in a most pitiable condition. He had been laid up with the grip. His place was untidy, his dishes were unwashed, and his fuel was running short. His appearance, in fact, rather frightened me. So I bundled him up and got him in the jumper and brought him straight home with me. He had a chill on the way, so as soon as we got to Casa Grande I sent him to bed, gave him hot whisky, and put my hot water bottle at his feet. He tried to accept the whole thing as a joke, and vowed I was jolly well cooking him. But to-night he has a high fever and I'm afraid he's in for a serious siege of illness. I intend to send Olie over to get some of his things and have his live stock brought over with ours.

Sunday the Twentieth

Percy has had three very bad nights, but seems a little better to-day. His lung is congested, and it may be pneumonia, but I think my mustard-plaster saved the day. He tries so hard to be cheerful, and is so grateful for every little thing. But I wish Dinky-Dunk was here to tell me what to do.

I could never have survived this last week without Olie. He is as watchful and ready as a farm-collie. But I want my Dinky-Dunk! I may have spoiled my Dinky-Dunk a little, but it's only once every century or two that God makes a man like him. I want to be a good wife. I want to do my share, and keep a shoulder to the wheel, if the going's got to be heavy for the next year or two. I won't be the Dixon type. I won't—I won't! My Duncan will need me during this next year, and it will be a joy to help him. For I love that man, Matilda Anne,—I love him so much that it hurts!

Sunday the Twenty-seventh

Christmas has come and gone. It was very lonely at Casa Grande. I prefer not writing about it. Percy is improving, but is still rather weak. I think he had a narrow squeak.

Wednesday the Thirtieth

My patient is up and about, looking like a different man. He shows the effects of my forced feeding, though he declares I'm trying to make him into a Strasburg goose, for the sake of the *pâté de foies gras* when I cut him up. But he's decided to go to Santa Barbara for the winter: and I think he's wise. So this afternoon I togged out in my furs, took the jumper, and went kiting over to the Titchborne Ranch. Oh, what a shack! What disorder, what untidiness, what spirit-numbing desolation! I don't blame poor Percival Benson for clearing out for California. I got what things he needed, however, and went kiting home again.

Thursday the Thirty-first

I hardly know how to begin. But it must be written or I'll suddenly go mad and start to bite the shack walls. Last night, after Percy had helped me turn the bread-mixer (for, whatever happens, we've at least got to eat) I helped him pack. Among other things, he found a copy of Housman's *Shropshire Lad* and after running through it announced that he'd like to read me two or three little things out of it. So I squatted down in front of the fire, idly poking at the red coals, and he sat beside the stove with his book, in slippers and dressing gown. And there he was solemnly reading out loud when the door opened and in walked Dinky-Dunk.

I say he walked in, but that isn't quite right. He stood in the open door, staring at us, with an expression that would have done credit to the Tragic Muse. I imagine Enoch Arden wore much the same look when he piped the home circle after that prolonged absence of his. Then Dinky-Dunk did a most unpardonable thing. Instead of saying "Howdy!" like a scholar and a gentleman, he backed out of the shack and slammed the door. When I'd caught my breath I went out through that door after him. It was a bitterly cold night, but I did not stop to put anything on. I was too amazed, too indignant, too swept off my feet by the absurdity of it all. I could see Dinky-Dunk in the clear starlight, taking the blankets off his team. He'd hurried to the shack, without even unharnessing the horses. I could hear the wheel-tires whine on the crisp snow, for the poor beasts were tired and restless. I went straight to the buckboard into which Dinky-Dunk was climbing. He looked like a cinnamon-bear in his big shaggy coat. And I couldn't see his face. But I remembered how it had looked in the doorway. It was the color of a tan shoe. It was too weather-beaten and burnt with the wind and sun-glare ever to turn white, or, I suppose, it would have been the color of paper.

"Haven't you," I demanded, "haven't you any explanation for acting like this?" He sat in the buckboard seat, with the reins in his hands.

"I guess I've got the first right to that question," he finally said in a stifled voice.

"Then why don't you ask it?" was my answer to him. Again he waited a moment before speaking, as though he felt the need of weighing his words.

"I don't need to—now!" he said, as he tightened the reins.

"Wait," I called out to him. "There are certain things I want you to know!"

I was not going to make explanations. I would not dignify his brute-man stupidity by such things. I scarcely know what I intended to do. As I looked up at him there in his rough fur coat, for a moment, he seemed millions and millions of miles away from me. I stared at him, trying to comprehend his utter lack of comprehension. I seemed to view him across the same gulf which separates a meditative zoo visitor from some abysmally hirsute animal that eons and eons ago must have been its cave-fellow and hearth-mate. But now we seemed to have nothing in common, not even a language with which to link up those lost ages. Yet from all that mixture of feelings only one survived: I didn't want my husband to go.

It was the team, as far as I can remember, that really decided the thing. They had been restive, backing and jerking and pawing and nickering for their feed-box. And suddenly they jumped forward. But this time they kept going. Whether Dinky-Dunk tried to hold them back or not I can't say. But I came back to the shack, shivering. Percy, thank Heaven, was in his room.

"I think I'll turn in!" he called out, quite casually, through the partition.

I said "All right," and sat down in front of the fire, trying to straighten things out. My Dinky-Dunk was gone! He had glared at me, with hate in his eyes, as he sat in that buckboard. It's all over. He has no faith in me, his own wife!

I went to bed and tried to sleep. But sleep was out of the question. The whole thing seemed so absurd, so unreasonable, so unjust. I could feel waves of anger sweep through my body at the mere thought of it. Then a wave of something else, of something between anxiety and terror, would take the place of anger. My husband was gone, and he'd never come back. I'd put all my eggs in one basket, and the basket had gone over, and made a saffron-tinted omelet of all my life.

And that's the way I watched the New Year in, I couldn't even afford the luxury of a little bawl, for I was afraid Percy would hear me. It must have been almost morning when I fell asleep.

When I woke up Percival Benson was gone, bag and baggage. At first I resented the thought of his going off that way, without a word, but on thinking it over I decided he'd done the right thing. There's nothing like the hard cold light of a winter morning to bring you back to hard cold facts. Olie had driven Percy in to the station. So I was alone in the shack all day. I did a heap of thinking during those long hours of solitude. And out of all that straw of self-examination I threshed just one little grain of truth. *I could never live on the prairie alone.* And whatever I did, or wherever I went, I could never be happy without my Dinky-Dunk....

I had just finished supper to-night, as blue as indigo and as spiritless as a wet hen, when I heard the sound of voices. It took me only ten seconds to make sure whose they were. Dinky-Dunk had come back with Olie! I made a high dive for a book from the nearest shelf, swung the armchair about with a jerk, and sank luxuriously into it, with my feet up on the warm damper and my eyes leisurely and contentedly perusing George Moore's *Confessions of a Young Man* (although I *hate* the libidinous stuff like poison!) Then Dinky-Dunk came in. I could see him stare at me a little awkwardly and contritely (what woman can't read a book and study a man at the same time?) and I, could see that he was waiting for an opening. But I gave him none. Naturally, Olie had explained everything to him. But I had been humiliated, my pride had been walked over, from end to end. My spirit had been stamped on—and I had decided on my plan of action. I simply ignored Duncan.

I read for a while, then I took a lamp, went to my room, and deliberately locked the door. My one regret was that I couldn't see Dinky-Dunk's face when that key turned. And now I must stop writing, and go to bed, for I am dog-tired. I know I'll sleep better to-night. It's nice to remember there's a man near, if he happens to be the man you care a trifle about, even though you *have* calmly turned the door-key on him.

Sunday the Third

Dinky-Dunk has at least the sensibilities to respect my privacy of life. He knows where the deadline is, and doesn't disregard it. But it's terribly hard to be tragic in a two-by-four shack. You miss the dignifying touches. And you haven't much leeway for the bulky swings of grandeur.

For one whole day I didn't speak to Dinky-Dunk, didn't even so much as recognize his existence. I ate by myself, and did my work—when the monster was around—with all the preoccupation of a sleep-walker. But something happened, and I forgot myself. Before I knew it I was asking him a question. He answered it, quite soberly, quite casually. If he had grinned, or shown one jot of triumph, I would have walked out of the shack and never spoken to him again. I think he knew he was on terribly perilous ground. He picked his way with care. He asked me a question back, quite offhandedly, and for the time being let the matter rest there. But the breach was in my walls, Matilda Anne, and I was quite defenseless. We were both very impersonal and very polite, when he came in at supper time, though I think I turned a visible pink when I sat down at the table, for our eyes met there, just a moment and no more. I knew he was watching me, covertly, all the time. And I knew I was making him pretty miserable. But I wasn't the least bit ashamed of it.

After supper he indifferently announced that he had nothing to do and might as well help me wash up. I went to hand him a dish-towel. Instead of taking the towel he took my hand, with the very profane ejaculation, as he did so, of "Oh, hell, Gee-Gee, what's the use?"

Then before I knew it, he had me in his arms (our butter-dish was broken in the collision) and I was weak enough to feel sorry for him and his poor tragic pleading eyes. Then I gave up. If I was silly enough to have a little cry on his shoulder, I had the satisfaction of feeling him give a gulp or two himself.

"You're the most wonderful woman in the world!" he solemnly told me, and then in a much less solemn way he began kissing me again. But the barriers were down. And how we talked that night! And how different everything seemed! And how nice it was to feel his arm over my shoulder and his quiet breathing on the nape of my neck as I fell asleep. It seemed as though Love were fanning me with its softest wings. I'm happy again. But I've been wondering if it's environment that makes character, or character that makes environment. Sometimes I think it's one way, and sometimes I feel it's the other. But I can't be sure of my answer—yet! It's hard for a spoiled woman to remember that her life has to be merged into somebody else's life. I've been wondering if marriage isn't like a two-panel screen, which won't stand up if both its panels are too much in line. Heaven knows, I want harmony! But a woman likes to feel that instead of being out of step with her whole regiment of life it's the regiment that's out of step with her. To-night I unlaced Dinky-Dunk's shoes, and put on his slippers, and sat on the floor between his knees with my head against the steady *tick-tock* of his watch-pocket. "Dinky-Dunk," I solemnly announced, "that gink called Pope was a poor guesser. The proper study of man should have been *woman*!"

Thursday the Seventh

Everything at Casa Grande has settled back into the usual groove. There is a great deal to do about the shack. The grimmest bug-bear of domestic work is dish-washing. A pile of greasy plates is the one thing that gets on my nerves. And it is a little Waterloo that must be faced three times every day, of every week, of every month, of every year. And I was never properly "broke" for domesticity and the dish-pan! Why can't some genius invent a self-washing fry-pan? My hair is growing so long that I can now do it up in a sort of half-hearted French roll. It has been quite cold, with a wonderful fall of snow. The sleighing could not be better.

Saturday the Ninth

Dinky-Dunk's Christmas present came to-day, over two weeks late. He had never mentioned it, and I had not only held my peace, but had given up all thought of getting a really-truly gift from my lord and master.

They brought it out from Buckhorn, in the bobsleigh, all wrapped up in old buffalo-robes and blankets and tarpaulins. *It's a baby-grand piano*, and a beauty, and it came all the way from Winnipeg. But either the shipping or the knocking about or the extreme cold has put it terribly out of tune, and it can't be used until the piano-tuner travels a couple of hundred miles out here to put it in shape. And it's far too big for the shack, even when pushed right up into the corner. But Dinky-Dunk says that before next winter there'll be a different sort of house on this spot where Casa Grande now stands.

"And that's to keep your soul alive, in the meantime," he announced. I scolded him for being so extravagant, when he needed every dollar he could lay his hands on. But he wouldn't listen to me. In fact, it only started an outburst.

"My God, Gee-Gee," he cried, "haven't you given up enough for me? Haven't you sacrificed enough in coming out here to the end of nowhere and leaving behind everything that made life decent?"

"Why, Honey Chile, didn't I get *you*?" I demanded. But even that didn't stop him.

"Don't you suppose I ever think what it's meant to you, to a woman like you? There are certain things we can't have, but there are some things we're going to have. This next ten or twelve months will be hard, but after that there's going to be a change—if the Lord's with me, and I have a white man's luck!"

"And supposing we have bad luck?" I asked him. He was silent for a moment or two.

"We can always give up, and go back to the city," he finally said.

"Give up!" I said with a whoop. "Give up? Not on your life, Mister Dour Man! We're not going to be Dixonites! We're going to win out!" And we were together in a death-clinch, hugging the breath out of each other, when Olie came in to ask if he hadn't better get the stock stabled, as there was bad weather coming.

Monday the Eleventh

We are having the first real blizzard of the winter. It began yesterday, as Olie intimated, and for all the tail-end of the day my Dinky-Dunk was on the go, in the bitter cold, looking after fuel and feed and getting things ship-shape, for all the world like a skipper who's read his barometer and seen a hurricane coming. There had been no wind for a couple of days, only dull and heavy skies with a disturbing sense of quietness. Even when I heard Olie and Dinky-Dunk shouting outside, and shoring up the shack-walls with poles, I could not quite make out what it meant.

Then the blizzard came. It came down out of the northwest, like a cloudburst. It hummed and sang, and then it whined, and then it screamed, screamed in a high falsetto that made you think poor old Mother Earth was in her last throes! The snow was fine and hard, really minute particles of ice, and not snow at all, as we know it in the East, little sharp-angled diamond-points that stung the skin like fire. It came in almost horizontal lines, driving flat across the unbroken prairie and defying anything made of God or man to stop it. Nothing did stop it. Our shack and the bunk-house and stables and hay-stacks tore a few pin-feathers off its breast, though; and those few feathers are drifts higher than my head, heaped up against each and all of the buildings.

I scratched the frost off a window-pane, where feathery little drifts were seeping in through the sill-cracks, when it first began. But the wind blew harder and harder and the shack rocked and shook with the tension. Oh, such a wind! It made a whining and wailing noise, with each note higher, and when you felt that it couldn't possibly increase, that it simply *must* ease off, or the whole world would go smash, why, that whining note merely grew tenser and the wind grew stronger. How it lashed things! How it shook and flailed and trampled this poor old earth of ours! Just before supper Olie announced that he'd look after my chicks for me. I told him, quite casually, that I'd attend to them myself. I usually strew a mixture of wheat and oats on the litter in the hen-house overnight. This had two advantages, one was that it didn't take me out quite so early in the morning, and the other was that the chicks themselves started scratching around first thing in the morning and so got exercise and kept themselves warmer-bodied and in better health.

It was not essential that I should go to the hen-house myself, but I was possessed with a sudden desire to face that singing white tornado. So I put on my things, while Dinky-Dunk was at work in the stables. I put on furs and leggings and gauntlets and all, as though I were starting for a ninety-mile drive, and slipped out. Dinky-Dunk had tunneled through the drift in front of the door, but that tunnel was already beginning to fill again. I plowed through it, and tried to look about me. Everything was a sort of streaked misty gray, an all-enveloping muffing leaden maelstrom that hurt your skin when you lifted your head and tried to look it in the face. Once, in a lull of the wind when the snow was not so thick, I caught sight of the hay-stacks. That gave me a line on the hen-house. So I made for it, on the run, holding my head low as I went.

It was glorious, at first, it made my lungs pump and my blood race and my legs tingle. Then the storm-devils howled in my eyes and the ice-lashes snapped in my face. Then the wind went off on a rampage again, and I couldn't see. I couldn't move forward. I couldn't even breathe. Then I got frightened.

I leaned there against the wind calling for Dinky-Dunk and Olie, whenever I could gasp breath enough to make a sound. But I might as well have been a baby crying in mid-ocean to a Kensington Gardens nurse.

Then I knew I was lost. No one could ever hear me in that roar. And there was nothing to be seen, just a driving, blinding, stinging gray pall of flying fury that nettled the naked skin like electric-massage and took the breath out of your buffeted body. There was no land-mark, no glimpse of any building, nothing whatever to go by. And I felt so helpless in the face of that wind! It seemed to take the power of locomotion from my legs. I was not altogether amazed at the thought that I might die there, within a hundred yards of my own home, so near those narrow walls within which were warmth, and shelter, and quietness. I imagined how they'd find my body, deep under the snow, some morning; how Dinky-Dunk would search, perhaps for days. I felt so sorry for him I decided not to give up, that I wouldn't be lost, that I wouldn't die there like a fly on a sheet of tanglefoot!

I had fallen down on my knees, with my back to the wind, and already the snow had drifted around me. I also found my eye-lashes frozen together, and I lost several winkers in getting rid of those solidified tears. But I got to my feet and battled on, calling when I could. I kept on, going round and round in a circle, I suppose, as people always do when they're lost in a storm. Then the wind grew worse again. I couldn't make any headway against it. I had to give up. I simply *had* to! I wasn't afraid. I wasn't terrified at the thought of what was happening to me. I was only sorry, with a misty sort of sorrow I can't explain. And I don't remember that I felt particularly uncomfortable, except for the fact I found it rather hard to breathe.

It was Olie who found me. He came staggering through the snow with extra fuel for the bunk-house, and nearly walked over me. As we found out afterward, I wasn't more than thirty steps away from that bunk-house door. Olie pulled me up out of the snow the same as you'd pull a skein of darning-silk out of a work-basket. He half carried me to the bunk-house, got his bearings, and then steered me for the shack. It was a fight, but we made it. And Dinky-Dunk was still out looking after his stock and doesn't know how nearly he lost his Lady Bird. I've made Olie promise not to say a word about it. But the top of my nose is red and swollen. I think it must have got a trifle frost-nipped, in the encounter. The weather has cleared now, and the wind has gone down. But it is very cold, and Dinky-Dunk has just reported that it's already forty-eight below zero.

Tuesday the Nineteenth

The days slip away and I scarcely know where they go. The weather is wonderful. Clear and cold, with such heaps of sunshine you'd never dream it was zero weather. But you have to be careful, and always wear furs when you're driving, or out for any length of time. Three hours in this open air is as good as a pint of Chinkie's best champagne. It makes me tingle. We are living high, with several barrels of frozen game—geese, duck and prairie-chicken—and also an old tin trunk stuffed full of beef-roasts, cut the right size. I bring them in and thaw them out overnight, as I need them. The freezing makes them very tender. But they must be completely thawed before they go into the oven, or the outside will be overdone and the inside still raw. I learned that by experience. My appetite is disgraceful, and I'm still gaining. Chinkie could never again say I reminded him of one of the lean kine in Pharaoh's dream.

I have been asking Dinky-Dunk if it isn't downright cruelty to leave horses and cattle out on the range in weather like this. My husband says not, so long as they have a wind-break in time of storms. The animals paw through the snow for grass to eat, and when they get thirsty they can eat the snow itself, which, Dinky-Dunk solemnly assures me, almost never gives them sore throat! But the open prairie, just at this season, is a most inhospitable looking pasturage, and the unbroken glare of white makes my eyes ache.... There's one big indoor task I finally have accomplished, and that is tuning my piano. It made my heart heavy, standing there useless, a gloomy monument of ironic grandeur.

As a girl I used to watch Katrinka's long-haired Alsatian putting her concert grand to rights, and I knew that my ear was dependable enough. So the second day after my baby grand's arrival I went at it with a monkey-wrench. But that was a failure. Then I made a drawing of a tuning-hammer and had Olie secretly convey it to the Buckhorn blacksmith, who in turn concocted a great steel hollow-headed monstrosity which actually fits over the pins to which the piano wires are strung, even though the aforesaid monstrosity is heavy enough to stun an ox with. But it did the work, although it took about two half-days, and now every note is true. So now I have music! And Dinky-Dunk does enjoy my playing, these long winter evenings. Some nights we let Olie come in and listen to the concert. He sits rapt, especially when I play ragtime, which seems the one thing that touches his holy of holies. Poor Olie! I surely have a good friend in that silent, faithful, uncouth Swede!

Dinky-Dunk himself is so thin that it worries me. But he eats well and doesn't anathematize my cooking. He's getting a few gray hairs, at the temples. I think they make him look rather *distingue*. But they worry my poor Dinky-Dunk. "Hully Gee," he said yesterday, studying himself for the third time in his shaving-glass, "I'm getting old!" He laughed when I started to whistle "Believe me if all those endearing young charms, which I gaze on so fondly to-day," but at heart he was really disturbed by the discovery of those few white hairs. I've been telling him that the ladies won't love him any more, and that his cut-up days are over. He says I'll have to make up for the others. So I started for him with my Australian crawl-stroke. It took me an hour to get the taste of shaving soap out of my mouth. Dinky-Dunk says I'm so full of life that I *sparkle*. All I know is that I'm happy, supremely and ridiculously happy!

Sunday the Thirty-first

The inevitable has happened. I don't know how to write about it! I *can't* write about it! My heart goes down like a freight elevator, slowly, sickeningly, even when I think about it. Dinky-Dunk came in and saw me studying a little row of dates written on the wall-paper beside the bedroom window. I pretended to be draping the curtain. "What's the matter, Lady Bird?" he demanded when he saw my face. I calmly told him that nothing was the matter. But he wouldn't let me go. I wanted to be alone, to think things out. But he kept holding me there, with my face to the light. I suppose I must have been all eyes, and probably shaking a little. And I didn't want him to suspect.

"Excuse me if I find you unspeakably annoying!" I said in a voice that was so desperately cold that it even surprised my own ears. He dropped me as though I had been a hot potato. I could see that I'd hurt him, and hurt him a lot. My first impulse was to run to him with a shower of repentant kisses, as one usually does, the same as one sprinkles salt on claret stains. But in him I beheld the original and entire cause—and I just couldn't do it. He called me a high-spirited devil with a hair-trigger temper. But he left me alone to think things out.

Tuesday the Ninth

I've started to say my prayers again. It rather frightened Dinky-Dunk, who sat up in bed and asked me if I wasn't feeling well. I promptly assured him that I was in the best of health. He not only agreed with me, but said I was as plump as a partridge. When I am alone, though, I get frightened and fidgety. So I kneel down every night and morning now and ask God for help and guidance. I want to be a good woman and a better wife. But I shall never let Duncan know—never!

Wednesday the Seventeenth

Do you remember Aunt Harriet who always wept when she read *The Isles of Greece?* She didn't even know where they were, and had never been east of Salem. But all the Woodberrys were like that. Dinky-Dunk came in and found me crying to-day, for the second time in one week. He made such valiantly ponderous efforts to cheer me up, poor boy, and shook his head and said I'd soon be an improvement on the Snider System, which is a system of irrigation by spraying overnight from pipes! My nerves don't seem so good as they were. The winter's so long. I'm already counting the days to spring.

Thursday the Twenty-fifth

Dinky-Dunk has concluded that I'm too much alone; he's been worrying over it. I can tell that. I try not to be moody, but sometimes I simply can't help it. Yesterday afternoon he drove up to Casa Grande, proud as Punch, with a little black and white kitten in the crook of his arm. He'd covered twenty-eight miles of trail for that kitten! It's to be my companion. But the kitten's as lonesome as I am, and has been crying, and nearly driving me crazy.

Tuesday the Second

The weather has been bad, but winter is slipping away. Dinky-Dunk has been staying in from his work, these mornings, helping me about the house. He is clumsy and slow, and has broken two or three of the dishes. But I hate to say anything; his eyes get so tragic. He declares that as soon as the trails are passable he's going to have a woman to help me, that this sort of thing can't go on any longer. He imagines it's merely the monotony of housework that is making my nerves so bad.

Yesterday morning I was drying the dishes and Dinky-Dunk was washing. I found the second spoon with egg on it. I don't know why it was, but that trivial streak of yellow along the edge of a spoon suddenly seemed to enrage me. It became monumental, an emblem of vague incapabilities which I would have to face until the end of my days. I flung that spoon back in the dish-pan. Then I turned on my husband and called out to him, in a voice that didn't quite seem like my own, "O God, can't you wash 'em *clean*? Can't you wash 'em clean?" I even think I ran up and down the room and pretty well made what Percival Benson would call "a bally ass" of myself. Dinky-Dunk didn't even answer me. But he dried his hands and got his things and went outdoors, to the stables, I suppose. His face was as colorless as it could possibly get. I felt sorry; but it was too late. And my sniffling didn't do any good. And it startled me, as I sat thinking things over, to realize that I'd lost my sense of humor.

Thursday the Fourth

Dinky-Dunk thinks I'm mad. I'm quite sure he does. He came in at noon to-day and found me on the floor with the kitten. I'd tied a piece of fur to the end of a string. Oh, how that kitten scrambled after that fur, round and round in a circle until he'd tumble over on his own ears! I was squeaking and weak with laughing when Dinky-Dunk stood in the door. Poor boy, he takes things so solemnly! But I know he thinks I'm quite mad. Perhaps I am. I cried myself to sleep last night. And for several days now I've had a longing for *caviare*.

Wednesday the Seventeenth

Spring is surely coming. It promises to be an early one. I feel better at the thought of it, and of getting out again. But the roads are quite impassable. Such mud! Such oceans of glue-pot dirt! They have a saying out here that soil is as rich as it is sticky. If this is true Dinky-Dunk has a second Garden of Eden. This mud sticks to everything, to feet, to clothes, to wagon-wheels. But there's getting to be real warmth in the sun that shines through my window.

Saturday the Twenty-seventh

A warm Chinook has licked up the last of the snow. Even Dinky-Dunk admits that spring is coming. For three solid hours an awakened blue-bottle has been buzzing against the pane of my bedroom window. I wonder if most of us aren't like that fly, mystified by the illusion of light that fails to lead to liberty? This morning I caught sight of Dinky-Dunk in his fur coat, climbing into the buckboard. I shall always hate to see him in that rig. It makes me think of a certain night. And we hate to have memory put a finger on our mental scars. When I was a girl Aunt Charlotte's second fiend of a husband locked me up in that lonely Derby house of theirs because I threw pebbles at the swans. Then off they drove to dinner somewhere and left me a prisoner there, where I sat listening to the bells of All Saints as the house gradually grew dark. And ever since then bells at evening have made me feel lonely and left me unhappy.

But the renaissance of the buckboard means that spring is here again. And for my Dinky-Dunk that means harder work. He's what they call a "rustler" out here. He believes in speed. He doesn't even wait until the frost is out of the ground before he starts to seed—just puts a drill over a two-inch batter of thawed-out mud, he's so mad about getting early on the land. He says he wants early wheat or no wheat. But he has to have help, and men are almost impossible to get. He had hoped for a gasoline tractor, but it can't be financed this spring, he has confessed to me. And I know, in my secret heart of hearts, that the tractor would have been here if it hadn't been for my piano!

There are still hundreds and hundreds of acres of prairie sod to "break" for spring wheat. Dinky-Dunk declares that he's going to risk everything on wheat this year. He says that by working two outfits of horses he himself can sow forty acres a day, but that means keeping the horses on the trot part of the time. He is thinking so much about his crop that I accused him of neglecting me.

"Is the varnish starting to wear off?" I inquired with a secret gulp of womanish self-pity. He saved the day by declaring I was just as crazy and just as adorable as I ever was. Then he asked me, rather sadly, if I was bored. "Bored?" I said, "how could I be bored with all these discomforts? No one is ever bored until they are comfortable!" But the moment after I'd said it I was sorry.

Tuesday the Sixth

Spring is here, with a warm Chinook creeping in from the Rockies and a sky of robin-egg blue. The gophers have come out of their winter quarters and are chattering and racing about. We saw a phalanx of wild geese going northward, and Dinky-Dunk says he's seen any number of ducks. They go in drifting V's, and I love to watch them melt in the sky-line. The prairie floor is turning to the loveliest of greens, and it is a joy just to be alive. I have been out all afternoon. The gophers aren't going to get ahead of me!

Monday the Twelfth

What would you say if you saw Brunhild drive up to your back door? What would you do if you discovered a Norse goddess placidly surveying you from a green wagon-seat? How would you act if you beheld a big blonde Valkyr suddenly introducing herself into your little earthly affairs?

Well, can you wonder that I stared, all eyes, when Dinky-Dunk brought home a figure like this, in the shape of a Finn girl named Olga Sarristo? Olga is to work in the fields, and to help me when she has time. But I'll never get used to having a Norse Legend standing at my elbow, for Olga is the most wonderful creature I have ever clapped eyes on. I say that without doubt, and without exaggeration. And what made the picture complete, she came driving a yoke of oxen—for Dinky-Dunk will have need of every horse and hauling animal he can lay his hands on. I simply held my breath as I stared up at her, high on her wagon-seat, blocked out in silhouette against the pale sky-line, a Brunhild with cowhide boots on. She wore a pale blue petticoat and a Swedish looking black shawl with bright-colored flowers worked along the hem. She had no hat. But she had two great ropes of pale gold hair, almost as thick as my arm, and hanging almost as low as her knees. She looked colossal up on the wagon-seat, but when she got down on the ground she was not so immense. She is, however, a strapping big woman, and I don't think I ever saw such shoulders! She is Olympian, Titanic! She makes me think of the Venus de Milo; there's such a largeness and calmness and smoothness of surface about her. I suppose a Saint-Gaudens might say that her mouth was too big and a Gibson might add that her nose hadn't the narrow rectitude of a Greek statue's, but she's a beautiful, a beautiful—"woman" was the word I was going to write, but the word "animal" just bunts and shoves itself in, like a stabled cow insisting on its own stall. But if you regard her as only animal, you must at least accept her as a perfect one. Her mouth is large, but I never saw such red lips, full and red and dewy. Her forehead is low and square, but milky smooth, and I know she could crack a chicken-bone between those white teeth of hers. Even her tongue, I noticed, is a watermelon red. She must be healthy. Dinky-Dunk says she's a find, that she can drive a double-seeder as well as any man in the West, and that by taking her for the season he gets the use of the ox-team as well. He warned me not to ask her about her family, as only a few weeks ago her father and younger brother were burned to death in their shack, a hundred miles or so north of us.

Tuesday the Twentieth

Olga has been with us a week, and she still fascinates me. She is installed in the annex, and seems calmly satisfied with her surroundings. She brought everything she owns tied up in an oat-sack. I have given her a few of my things, for which she seems dumbly grateful. She seldom talks, and never laughs. But I am teaching her to say "yes" instead of "yaw." She studies me with her limpid blue eyes, and if she is silent she is never sullen. She hasn't the heavy forehead and jaw of the Galician women and she hasn't the Asiatic cast of face that belongs to the Russian peasant. And she has the finest mouthful of teeth I ever saw in a human head—and she never used a toothbrush in her life! She is only nineteen, but such a bosom, such limbs, such strength!

This is a great deal of talk about Olga, I'm afraid, but you must remember that Olga is an event. I expected Olie would be keeled over by her arrival, but they seem to regard each other with silent contempt. I suppose that is because racially and physically they are of the same type. I'm anxious to see what Percival Benson thinks of Olga when he gets back—they would be such opposites. Olga is working with her ox-team on the land. Two days ago I rode out on Paddy and watched her. There was something Homeric about it, something Sorolla would have jumped at. She seemed so like her oxen. She moved like them, and her eyes were like theirs. She has the same strength and solemnity when she walks. She's so primitive and natural and instinctive in her actions. Yesterday, after dinner, she curled up on a pile of hay at one end of the corral and fell asleep for a few minutes, flat in the strong noonday light. I saw Dinky-Dunk stop on his way to the stable and stand and look down at her. I slipped out beside him. "God, what a woman!" he said under his breath. A vague stab of jealousy went through me as I heard him say that. Then I looked at her hand, large, relaxed, roughened with all kinds of weather and calloused with heavy work. And this time it was an equally vague stab of pity that went through me.

Monday the Twenty-sixth

The rush is on, and Dinky-Dunk is always out before six. If it's true, as some one once said, that the pleasures of life depended on its anxieties, then we ought to be a hilarious household. Every one is busy, and I do what I can to help. I don't know why it is, but I find an odd comfort in the thought of having another woman near me, even Olga. She also helps me a great deal with the housework. Those huge hands of hers have a dexterity you'd never dream of. She thinks the piano a sort of miracle, and me a second miracle for being able to play it. In the evening she sits back in a corner, the darkest corner she can find, and listens. She never speaks, never moves, never expresses one iota of emotion. But in the gloom I can often catch the animal-like glow of her eyes. They seem almost phosphorescent. Dinky-Dunk had a long letter from Percival Benson to-day. It was interesting and offhandedly jolly and just the right sort. And Percy says he'll be back on the Titchborne place in a few weeks.

Wednesday the Twenty-eighth

Olga went through the boards of her wagon-box and got a bad scrape on her leg. She showed me the extent of her injuries, without the slightest hesitation, and I gave her first-aid treatment with my carbolated vaseline. And still again I had to think of the Venus de Milo, for it was a knee like a statue's, milky white and round and smooth, with a skin like a baby's, and so different to her sunburnt forearms. It was Olympian more than Fifth-Avenuey. It was a leg that made me think, not of Rubens, but of Titian, and my thoughts at once went out to the right-hand lady of the "Sacred and Profane Love," in the Borghese, there was such softness and roundness combined with its strength. And Dinky-Dunk walked in and stood staring at it, himself, with never so much as a word of apology. Olga looked up at him without a flicker of her ox-like eyes. It wasn't until I made an angry motion for her to drop her skirt that she realized any necessity for covering the Titian knee. But again I felt that odd pang of jealousy needle through me as I saw his face. At least I suppose it was jealousy, the jealousy of an artful little Mona-Lisa minx who didn't even class in with the demigods. When Olga was gone, however, I said to Dinky-Dunk: "Isn't that a limb for your life?"

He merely said: "We don't grow limbs up here, Tabby. They're legs, just plain legs!"

"Anything but *plain*!" I corrected him. Then he acknowledged that he'd seen those knees before. He'd stumbled on Olga and her brother knee-deep in mud and cow manure, treading a mixture to plaster their shack with, the same as the Doukhobors do. It left me less envious of those Junoesque knees.

Monday the Second

Keeping chickens is a much more complicated thing than the outsider imagines. For example, several of my best hens, quite untouched by the modern spirit of feminine unrest, have been developing "broodiness" and I have been trying to "break them up," as the poulterers put it. But they are determined to set. This mothering instinct is a fine enough thing in its way, but it's been spoiling too many good eggs. So I've been trying to emancipate these ruffled females. I lift them off the nest by the tail feathers, ten times a day. I fling cold water in their solemn maternal faces. I put little rings of barb-wire under their sentimental old bosoms. But still they set. And one, having pecked me on the wrist until the blood came, got her ears promptly boxed—in face of the fact that all poultry keepers acknowledge that kindness to a hen improves her laying qualities.

Thursday the Fifth

Casa Grande is a beehive of industry. Every one has a part to play. I am no longer expected to sit by the fire and purr. At nights I sew. Dinky-Dunk is so hard on his clothes! When it's not putting on patches it's sewing on buttons. Then we go to bed at half-past nine. At half-past nine, think of it! Little me, who more than once went humming up Fifth Avenue when morning was showing gray over the East River, and often left Sherry's (oh, those dear old dancing days!) when the milk wagons were rumbling through Forty-fourth Street, and once triumphantly announced, on coming out of Dorlon's and studying the old Oyster-Letter clock, that I'd stuck it out to Y minutes past O! But it's no hardship to get up at five, these glorious mornings. The days get longer, and the weather is perfect. And the prairie looks as though a vacuum cleaner had been at work on it overnight. Positively, there's a charwoman who does this old world over, while we sleep! By morning it's as bright as a new pin. And out here every one is thinking of the day ahead; Dinky-Dunk, of his crop; Olga, of the pair of sky-blue corsets I've written to the Winnipeg mail-order house for; Olie, of the final waterproofing of the granaries so the wheat won't get spoilt any more; Gee-Gee, herself, of—of something which she's almost afraid to think about.

Dinky-Dunk, in his deviling moods, says I'm an old married woman now, that I'm settled, that I've eaten my pie! Perhaps I have. I'm not imaginative, so I must depend on others for my joy of living. I know now that I can never create, never really express myself in any way worth while, either on paper or canvas or keyboard. And people without imagination, I suppose, simply have to drop back to racial simplicities—which means I'll have to have a family, and feed hungry mouths, and keep a home going. And I'll have to get all my art at second-hand, from magazines and gramophone records and plaster-of-Paris casts. Just a housewife! And I so wanted to be something more, once! Yet I wonder if, after all, the one is so much better than the other? I wonder? And here comes my Dinky-Dunk, and in three minutes he'll be kissing me on the tip of the chin and asking me what there's going to be good for supper! And that is better than fame! For all afternoon those twelve little lines of Dobson's have been running through my head:

Fame is a food that dead men eat—I have no stomach for such meat.In little light and narrow rooms,They eat it in the silent tombs,With no kind voice of comrade nearTo bid the banquet be of cheer.

But Friendship is a noble thing—Of Friendship it is good to sing,For truly when a man shall end,He lives in memory of his friendWho doth his better part recallAnd of his faults make funeral!

But when you put the word "love" there instead of "friendship" you make it even better.... Olga, by the way, is not so stupid as you might imagine. She's discovered something which I didn't intend her to find out.... And Olie, also by the way, has solved the problem of "breaking up" my setting hens. He has made a swinging coop with a wire netting bottom, for all the world like the hanging gardens of Babylon, and into this all the ruffled mothers-to-be have been thrust and the coop hung up on the hen-house wall. Open wire is a very uncomfortable thing to set on, and these hens have at last discovered that fact. I have been out looking at them. I never saw such a parliament of solemn indignation. But their pride has been broken, and they are beginning to show a healthier interest in their meals.

Tuesday the Tenth

I've been wondering if Dinky-Dunk is going to fall in love with Olga. Yesterday I saw him staring at her neck. She's the type of woman that would really make the right sort of wilderness wife. She seems an integral part of the prairie, broad-bosomed, fecund, opulent. And she's so placid and large and soft-spoken and easy to live with. She has none of my moods and tantrums.

Her corsets came to-day, and I showed her how to put them on. She is incontinently proud of them, but in my judgment they only make her ridiculous. It's as foolish as putting a French *toque* on one of her oxen. The skin of Olga's great shoulders is as smooth and creamy as a baby's. I have been watching her eyes. They are not a dark blue, but in a strong side-light they seem deep wells of light, layer on layer of azure. And she is mysterious to me, calmly and magnificently inscrutable. And I once thought her an uncouth animal. But she is a great help. She has planted rows and rows of sweet peas all about Casa Grande and is starting to make a kitchen garden, which she's going to fence off and look after with her own hands. It will be twice the size of Olie's. But I do hope she doesn't ever grow into something mysterious to my Dinky-Dunk. This morning she said I ought to work in the garden, that the more I kept on my feet the better it would be for me later on.

As for Dinky-Dunk, the poor boy is working himself gaunt. Yet tired as he is, he tries to read a few pages of something worth while every night. Sometimes we take turns in reading. Last night he handed me over his volume of Spencer with a pencil mark along one passage. This passage said: "Intellectual activity in women is liable to be diminished after marriage by that antagonism between individuation and reproduction everywhere operative throughout the organic world." I don't know why, but that passage made me as hot as a hornet. In the background of my brain I carried some vague memory of George Eliot once catching this same philosophizing Spencer fishing with a composite fly, and, remarking on his passion for generalizations, declaring that he even fished with a generalization. So I could afford to laugh. "Spencer's idea of a tragedy," I told Dinky-Dunk, "is a deduction killed by a fact!" And again I smiled my Mona-Lisa smile. "And I'm going to be one of the facts!" I proudly proclaimed.

Dinky-Dunk, after thinking this over, broke into a laugh. "You know, Gee-Gee," he solemnly announced, "there are times when you seem almost clever!" But I wasn't clever in this case, for it was hours later before I saw the trap which Dinky-Dunk had laid for me!

Monday the Sixteenth

All day Saturday Olga and Dinky-Dunk were off in the chuck-wagon, working too far away to come home for dinner. The thought of them being out there, side by side, hung over me like a cloud. I remembered how he had absently stared at the white column of her neck. And I pictured him stopping in his work and studying her faded blue cotton waist pulled tight across the line of that opulent bust. What man wouldn't be impressed by such bodily magnificence, such lavish and undulating youth and strength? And there's something so soft and diffused about those ox-like eyes of hers! You do not think, then, of her eyes being such a pale blue, any more than you could stop to accuse summer moonlight of not being ruddy. And those unruffled blue eyes never seem to see you; they rather seem to bathe you in a gaze as soft and impersonal as moonlight itself.

I simply couldn't stand it any more. I got on Paddy and galloped out for my Dinky-Dunk, as though it were my sudden and solemn duty to save him from some imminent and awful catastrophe.

I stopped on the way, to watch a couple of prairie-chickens minuetting through the turns of their vernal courtships. The pompous little beggars with puffed-out wattles and neck ruffs were positively doing cancans and two-steps along the prairie floor. Love was in the air, that perfect spring afternoon, even for the animal world. So instead of riding openly and honestly up to Dinky-Dunk and Olga, I kept under cover as much as I could and stalked them, as though I had been a timber wolf.

Then I felt thoroughly and unspeakably ashamed of myself, for I caught sight of Olga high on her wagon, like a Valkyr on a cloud, and Dinky-Dunk hard at work a good two miles away.

He was a little startled to see me come cantering up on Paddy. I don't know whether it was silly or not, but I told him straight out what had brought me. He hugged me like a bear and then sat down on the prairie and laughed. "With that cow?" he cried. And I'm sure no man could ever call the woman he loves a cow.... I believe Dinky-Dunk suspects something. He's just asked me to be more careful about riding Paddy. And he's been more solemnly kind, lately. But I'll never tell him—never—never!

Tuesday the Twenty-fourth

Percy will be back to-morrow. It will be a different looking country to what it was when he left. I've been staring up at a cobalt sky, and begin to understand why people used to think Heaven was somewhere up in the midst of such celestial blue. And on the prairie the sky is your first and last friend. Wasn't it Emerson who somewhere said that the firmament was the daily bread for one's eyes? And oh, the lovely, greening floor of the wheat country now! Such a soft yellow-green glory stretching so far in every direction, growing so much deeper day by day! And the sun and space and clear light on the sky-line and the pillars of smoke miles away and the wonderful, mysterious promise that is hanging over this teeming, steaming, shimmering, abundant broad bosom of earth! It thrills me in a way I can't explain. By night and day, before breakfast and after supper, the talk is of wheat, wheat, wheat, until I nearly go crazy. I complained to Dinky-Dunk that he was dreaming wheat, living wheat, breathing wheat, that he and all the rest of the world seemed mad about wheat.

"And there's just one other thing you must remember, Lady Bird," was his answer. "All the rest of the world is *eating* wheat. It can't live without wheat. And I'd rather be growing the bread that feeds the hungry than getting rich making cordite and Krupp guns!" So he's risking everything on this crop of his, and is eternally figuring and planning and getting ready for the *grande débâcle*. He says it will be like a battle. And no general goes into a battle without being prepared for it. But when we read about the doings of the outside world, it seems like reading of happenings that have taken place on the planet Mars. We're our own little world just now, self-contained, rounded-out, complete.

Friday the Third

Two things of vast importance have happened. Dinky-Dunk has packed up and made off to Edmonton to interview some railway officials, and Percy is back. Dinky-Dunk is so mysteriously silent as to the matter of his trip that I'm afraid he is worried about money matters. And he asked me if I'd mind keeping the household expenses down as low as I could, without actual hardship, for the next few months.

As for Percy, he seemed a little constrained, but looked ever so much better. He is quite sunburned, likes California and says we ought to have a winter bungalow there (and Dinky-Dunk just warning me to save on the pantry pennies!) He's brought a fastidious little old English woman back with him as a housekeeper, a Mrs. Watson, and she looks both capable and practical. Notwithstanding the fact that she seems to have stepped right out of Dickens, and carries a huge Manx cat about with her, Percy said he thought they'd muddle along in some way. Thoughtful boy that he was, he brought me a portmanteau packed full of the newer novels and magazines, and a two-pound jar of smoking tobacco for Dinky-Dunk.

Thursday the Ninth

A Belasco couldn't have more carefully stage-managed the first meeting between Percy and Olga. I felt that she was my discovery, and I wanted to spring her on him, at the right moment, and in the right way. I wanted to get the Valkyr on a cloud effect. So I kept Percy in the house on the pretext of giving him a cup of tea, until I should hear the rumble of the wagon and know that Olga was swinging home with her team. It so happened, when I heard the first faint far thunder of that homing wagon, that Percy was sitting in my easy chair, with a cup of my thinnest china in one hand and a copy of Walter Pater's *Marius the Epicurean* in the other. We had been speaking of climate, and he wanted to look up the passage where Pater said, "one always dies of the cold"—which I consider a slur on the Northwest!

I couldn't help realizing, as I sat staring at Percy, at the thin, over-sensitive face, and the high-arched, over-refined nose, and the narrow, stooping, over-delicate shoulders, what a direct opposite he was to Olga, in every way. Instead of thin china and Pater in her hand at that very moment, I remembered she'd probably have a four-tined fork or a mud-stained fence stretcher.

I went to the door and looked out. At the proper moment I called Percy. Olga was standing up in the wagon-box, swinging about one corner of the corral. She stood with her shoulders well back, for her weight was already on the lines, to pull the team up. Her loose blue skirt edge was fluttering in the wind, but at the front was held tight against her legs, like the drapery of the Peace figure in the Sherman statue in the Plaza. Across that Artemis-like bosom her thin waist was stretched tight. She had no hat on, and her pale gold hair, which had been braided and twisted up into a heavy crown, had the sheen of metal on it, in the later afternoon sun. And in that clear glow of light, which so often plays mirage-like tricks with vision, she loomed up like a demi-god, or a she-Mercury who ought to have had little bicycle wheels attached to her heels.

Percy is never demonstrative. But I could see that he was more than impressed. He was amazed.

"My word!" he said very quietly.

"What does she make you think of?" I demanded.

Percy put down his teacup.

"Don't go away," I commanded, "but tell me what she makes you think of." He still stood staring at her with puckered up eyes.

"She's like band-music going by!" he proclaimed. "No, she's more than that; she's Wagner on wheels," he finally said. "No, not that! A Norse myth in dimity!"

I told him it wasn't dimity, but he was too interested in Olga to listen to me.

Half an hour later, when she met him, she was very shy. She turned an adorable pink, and then calmly rebuttoned the two top buttons of her waist, which had been hanging loose. And I noticed that Percy did precisely what I saw Dinky-Dunk once doing. He sat staring absently yet studiously at the milky white column of Olga's neck! And I had to speak to him twice, before he even woke up to the fact that he was being addressed by his hostess.

Wednesday the Fifteenth

Dinky-Dunk is back, and very busy again. During the day I scarcely get a glimpse of him, except at meal-times. I have a steadily growing sense of being neglected, but I know how a worried man hates petulance. The really important thing is that Percy is giving Olga lessons in reading and writing. For, although a Finn, she is a Canadian Finn from almost the shadow of the sub-Arctics, and has had little chance for education. But her mind is not obtuse.

Yesterday I asked Olga what she thought of Percival Benson. "Ah lak heem," she calmly admitted in her majestic, monosyllabic way. "He is a fonny leetle man." And the "fonny leetle man" who isn't really little, seems to like Olga, odd as it may sound. They are such opposites, such contradictions! Percy says she's Homeric. He says he never saw eyes that were so limpid, or such pools of peace and calm. He insists on the fact that she's essentially maternal, as maternal as the soil over which she walks, as Percy put it. I told him what Dinky-Dunk had once told me, about Olga killing a bull. The bull was a vicious brute that had attacked her father and knocked him down. He was striking at the fallen man with his fore-paws when Olga heard his cries. She promptly came for that bull with a pitchfork. And speaking of Homer, it must have been a pretty epical battle, for she killed the bull and left the fork-tines eight inches in his body while she picked up her father and carried him back to the house. And I won't even kill my own hens, but have always appointed Olie as the executioner.

Friday the Seventeenth

It is funny to see Percy teaching Olga. She watches him as though he were a miracle man. Her dewy red lips form the words slowly, and the full white throat utters them largely, laboriously, instruments on them, and in some perhaps uncouth way makes them lovely. I sit with my sewing, listening. Sometimes I open the piano and play. But I feel out of it. I seem to be on the fringe of things that are momentous only to other people. Last night, when Percy said he thought he'd sell his ranch, Dinky-Dunk looked up from his paper-littered desk and told him to hang on to that land like a leech. But he didn't explain why.

Saturday the Nineteenth

I can't even remember the date. But I know that midsummer is here, that the men folks are so busy I have to shift for myself, and that the talk is still of wheat, and how it's heading, and how the dry weather of the last few weeks will affect the length of the straw. Dinky-Dunk is making desperate efforts to get men to cut wild-hay. He's bought the hay rights of a large stretch between some sloughs about seven miles east of our place. He says men are scarcer than hen's teeth, but has the promise of a couple of cutthroats who were thrown off a freight-train near Buckhorn. Percy volunteered to help, and was convinced of the fact that he could drive a mower. Olie, who nurses a vast contempt for Percy, and, I secretly believe, rather resents his attentions to Olga, put the new team of colts on the mower. They promptly ran away with Percy, who came within an ace of being thrown in front of the mower-knife, which would have chopped him up into very unscholarly mincemeat. Olga got on a horse, bareback, and rounded up the colts. Then she cooed about poor bruised Percy and tried to coax him to come to the house. But Percy said he was going to drive that team, even if he had to be strapped to the mower-seat. And, oddly enough, he did "gat them beat," as Olga expressed it, but it tired him out and wilted his collar and the sweat was running down his face when he came in at noon. Olga is very proud of him. But she announced that she'd drive that mower herself, and sailed into Olie for giving a tenderfoot a team like that to drive. It was her first outburst. I couldn't understand a word she said, but I know that she was magnificent. She looked like a statue of Justice that had suddenly jumped off its pedestal and was doing its best to put a Daniel Webster out of business!

Friday the Twenty-eighth

The weather is still very dry. But Dinky-Dunk feels sure it will not affect his crop. He says the filaments of a wheat-plant will go almost two feet deep in search for moisture. Yesterday Percy appeared in a flannel shirt, and without his glasses. I think he is secretly practising calisthenics. He said he was going to cut out this afternoon tea, because it doesn't seem to fit in with prairie life. I fancy I see the re-barbarianizing influence of Olga at work on Percival Benson Woodhouse. Either Dinky-Dunk or Olie, I find, has hidden my saddle!

Saturday the Twenty-ninth

To-day has been one of the hottest days of the year. It may be good for the wheat, but I can't say that it seems good for me. All day long I've been fretting for far-away things, for foolish and impossible things. I tried reading Keats, but that only made me worse than ever. I've been longing for a glimpse of the Luxembourg Gardens in spring, with all the horse-chestnuts in bloom. I've been wondering how lovely it would be to drift into the Blue Grotto at Capri and see the azure sea-water drip from the trailing boat-oars. I've been burning with a hunger to see a New England orchard in the slanting afternoon sunlight of an early June afternoon. The hot white light of this open country makes my eyes ache and seems to dry my soul up. I can't help thinking of cool green shadows, and musky little valleys of gloom with a brook purling over mossy stones. I long for the solemn greenery of great elms, aisles and aisles of cathedral-like gloom and leaf-filtered sunlight. I'd love to hear an English cuckoo again, and feel the soft mild sea-air that blows up through Louis's dear little Devonshire garden. But what's the use!

I went to the piano and pounded out *Kennst Du Das Land* with all my soul, and I imagine it did me good. It at least bombarded the silence out of Casa Grande. The noise of life is so far away from you on the prairie! It is not utterly silent, just that dreamy and disembodied sigh of wind and grass against which a human call targets like a leaden bullet against metal. It is almost worse than silence.

Sunday the Thirtieth

My mood is over. Early, early this morning I slipped out of bed and watched day break. I saw the first faint orange rim along the limitless sky-line, and then the pearly pink above it, and all the sweet dimness and softness and mystery of God's hand pulling the curtains of morning apart. And then the rioting orchestras of color struck up, and I leaned out of the window bathed in glory as the golden disk of the sun showed over the dewy prairie-edge. Oh, the grandeur of it! And oh, the God-given freshness of that pellucid air! I love my land! I love it!

Tuesday the First

I have married a *man*! My Dinky-Dunk is not a softy. I had that proved to me yesterday, when I put Paddy in the buckboard and drove out to where the men were working in the hay. I was taking their dinner out to them, neatly packed in the chuck-box. One of the new men, who'd been hired for the rush, had been overworking his team. The brute had been prodding them with a pitchfork, instead of using a whip. Dinky-Dunk saw the marks, and noticed one of the horses bleeding. But he didn't interfere until he caught the man in the act of jabbing the tines into Maid Marian's flank. Then he jumped for him, just as I drove up. He cursed that man, cursed and damned him most dreadfully and pulled him down off the hay-rack. Then they fought.

They fought like two wildcats. Dinky-Dunk's nose bled and his lip was cut. But he knocked the other man flat, and when he tried to get up he knocked him again. It seemed cruel; it was revolting. But something in me rejoiced and exulted as I saw that hulk of an animal thresh and stagger about the hay-stubble. I tried to wipe the blood away from Dinky-Dunk's nose. But he pushed me back and said this was no place for a woman. I had no place in his universe, at that particular time. But Dinky-Dunk can fight, if he has to. He's sa magerful a mon! He's afraid of nothing.

But that was nearly a costly victory. Both the new men of course threw up their jobs, then and there. Dinky-Dunk paid them off, on the spot, and they started off across the open prairie, without even waiting for their meal. Dinky-Dunk, as we sat down on the dry grass and ate together, said it was a good riddance, and he was just saying I could only have the left-hand side of his mouth to kiss for the next week when he suddenly dropped his piece of custard-pie, stood up and stared toward the east. I did the same, wondering what had happened.

I could see a long thin slanting column of smoke driving across the hot noonday air. Then my heart stopped beating. *It was the prairie on fire.*

I had heard a great deal about fire-guards and fire-guarding, three rows about crops and ten about buildings; and I knew that Olie hadn't yet finished turning all those essential furrows. And if that column of smoke, which was swinging up through the silvery haze where the indigo vault of heaven melted into the dusty whiteness of the parched grasslands, had come from the mouth of a siege-gun which was cannonading us where we stood, it couldn't have more completely chilled my blood. For I knew that east wind would carry the line of fire crackling across the prairie floor to

Dinky-Dunk's wheat, to the stables and out-buildings, to Casa Grande itself, and all our scheming and planning and toiling and moiling would go up in one yellow puff of smoke. And once under way, nothing could stop that widening river of flame.

It was Dinky-Dunk who jumped to life as though he had indeed been cannonaded. In one bound he was at the buckboard and was snatching out the horse-blanket that lay folded up under the seat. Then he unsnapped the reins from Paddy's bridle, snapping them on the blanket, one to the buckle and the other to the strap-end. In another minute he had the hobble off Paddy and had swung me up on that astonished pinto's back. The next minute he himself was on Maid Marian, poking one end of the long rein into my hand and telling me to keep up with him.

We rode like mad. I scarcely understood what it meant, at the time, but I at least kept up with him. We went floundering through one end of a slough until the blanket was wet and heavy and I could hardly hold it. But I hung on for dear life. Then we swung off across the dry grass toward that advancing semicircle of fire, as far apart as the taut reins would let us ride. Dinky-Dunk took the windward side. Then on we rushed, along that wavering frontier of flame, neck to neck, dragging the wet blanket along its orange-tinted crest, flattening it down and wiping it out as we went. We made the full circle, panting; saw where the flames had broken out again, and swung back with our dragging blanket. But when one side was conquered another side would revive, and off we'd have to go again, until my arm felt as though it were going to be pulled out of its socket.

But we won that fight, in the end. I slipped down off Paddy's back and lay full length on the sod, weak, shaking, wondering why the solid ground was rocking slowly from side to side like a boat. But Dinky-Dunk didn't even observe me. He was fighting out the last patch of fire, on foot.

When he came over to where I was waiting for him he was as sooty and black as a boiler-maker. He dropped down beside me, breathing hard. We sat there holding each other's hand, for several minutes, in utter silence. Then he said, rather thickly: "Are you all right?" And I told him that of course I was all right. Then he said, without looking at me, "I forgot!" Then he got Paddy and patched up the harness and took me home in the buckboard.

But all the rest of the day he hung about the shack, as solemn as an owl. And once in the night he got up and lighted the lamp and came over and studied my face. I blinked up at him sleepily, for I was dog-tired and had been dreaming that we were back in Paris at the Bal des Quatz Arts and were about to finish up with an early breakfast at the Madrid. He looked so funny with his rumpled up hair and his faded pajamas that I couldn't help laughing a little as he blew out the light and got back into bed.

"Dinky-Dunk," I said, as I turned over my pillow and got comfy again, "wouldn't it have been hell if all our wheat had been burned up?" I forget what Duncan said, for in two minutes I was asleep again.

Monday the Seventh

The dry spell has been broken, and broken with a vengeance. One gets pretty well used to high winds, in the West. There used to be days at a time when that unending high wind would make me think something was going to happen, filling me with a vague sense of impending calamity and making me imagine a big storm was going to blow up and wipe Casa Grande and its little coterie off the map. But we've had a real wind-storm, this time, with rain and hail. Dinky-Dunk's wheat looks sadly draggled out and beaten down, but he says there wasn't enough hail to hurt anything; that the straw will straighten up again, and that this downpour was just what he wanted. Early in the afternoon, on looking out the shack door, I saw a tangle of clouds on the sky-line. They seemed twisted up like a skein of wool a kitten had been playing with. Then they seemed to marshal themselves into one solid line and sweep up over the sky, getting blacker and blacker as they came. Olga ran in with her yellow hair flying, slamming and bolting the stable-doors, locking the chicken-coop, and calling out for me to get my clothes off the line or they'd be blown to pieces. Even then I could feel the wind. It whipped my own hair loose, and flattened my skirt against my body, and I had to lean forward to make any advance against it.

By this time the black army of the heavens had rolled up overhead and a few big frog-like drops of rain began to fall, throwing up little clouds of dust, as a rifle bullet might. I trundled out a couple of tubs, in the hope of catching a little soft water. It wasn't until later that I realized the meaning of Olga's mild stare of reproof. For the next moment the downpour came, and with it the wind. And such wind! There had been nothing to stop its sweep, of course, for hundreds and hundreds of miles, and it hit us the same as a hurricane at sea hits a liner. The shack shook with the force of it. My two wash-tubs went bounding and careening off across the landscape, the chicken-coop went over like a nine-pin, and the air was filled with bits of flying timber. Olga's wagon, with the hay-rack on top of it, moved solemnly and ponderously across the barnyard and crashed into the corral, propelled by no power but that of the wind. My sweet-pea hedges were torn from their wires, and an armful of hay came smack against the shack-window and was held there by the wind, darkening the room more than ever.

Then the storm blew itself out, though it poured for two or three hours afterward. And all the while, although I exulted in that play of elemental force, I was worrying about my Dinky-Dunk, who was away for the day, doing what he could to arrange for some harvest hands, when the time for cutting came. For the wheat, it seems, ripens all at once, and then the grand rush begins. If it isn't cut the moment it's ripe, the grain shells out, and that means loss. Olga has been saying that the wheat on the Cummins section will easily run forty bushels to the acre and over. It will also grade high, whatever that means. There are six hundred and forty acres of it in that section, and I've just figured out that this means a little over twenty-five thousand bushels of grain. Our other piece on the home ranch is a larger tract, but a little lighter in crop. That wheat is just beginning to turn from green to the palest of yellow. And it has a good show, Olga says, if frost will only keep off and no hail comes. Our one occupation, for the next few weeks, will be watching the weather.

Sunday the Thirteenth

Percy and Mrs. Watson drove over to see how we'd all weathered the storm. They found the chicken-coop once more right side up, and everything ship-shape. Percy promptly asked where Olga was. I pointed her out to him, breast-high in the growing wheat. She looked like Ceres, in her big, new, loose-fitting blue waist, with the noonday sun on her yellow-gold head and her mild ruminative eyes with their misted sky-line effect. She always seems to fit into the landscape here. I suppose it's because she's a born daughter of the soil. And a sea of wheat makes a perfect frame for that massive, benignant figure of hers.

I looked at Percy, at thin-nosed, unpractical Percy, with all his finicky sensibilities, with his high fastidious reticences, with his effete, inbred meagerness of bone and sinew, with his distinguished pride of distinguished race rather running to seed. And I stood marveling at the wisdom of old Mother Nature, who was so plainly propelling him toward this revitalizing, revivifying, reanimalizing, redeeming type which his pale austerities of spirit could never quite neutralize. Even Dinky-Dunk has noticed what is taking place. He saw them standing side by side in the grain. When he came in he pointed them out to me, and merely said, "*Hermann und Dorothea*!" But I remembered my Goethe well enough to understand.

Monday the Twenty-eighth

I woke Dinky-Dunk up last night crying beside him in bed. I just got to thinking about things again, how far away we were from everything, how hard it would be to get help if we needed it, and how much I'd give if I only had you, Matilda Anne, for the next few weeks.... I got up and went to the window and looked out. The moon was big and yellow, like a cheese. And the midnight prairie itself seemed so big and wide and lonely, and I seemed such a tiny speck on its face, so far away from every one, from God himself, that the courage went out of my body like the air out of a tire. Dinky-Dunk was right; it is life that is taming me.

I stood at the window praying, and then I slipped back into bed. Dinky-Dunk works so hard and gets so tired that it would take a Chinese devil-gong to waken him, once he's asleep. He did not stir when I crept back into bed. And that, as I lay there wide awake, made me feel that even my own husband had betrayed me. And I *bawled*. I must have shaken the bed, for Dinky-Dunk finally did wake up. I couldn't tell him what was the matter. I blubbered out that I only wanted him to hold me. He took me in his arms and kissed my wet eyelids, hugging me up close to him, until I got quieter. Then I fell asleep. But poor Dinky-Dunk was awake when I opened my eyes about four, and had been that way for hours. He was afraid of disturbing me by taking his arm from under my head. To-day he looks tired and dark around the eyes. But he was up and off early. There is so much to be done these days! He is putting up a grub-tent and a rough sleeping-shack for the harvest "hands," so that I won't be bothered with a lot of rough men about the house here. I'm afraid I'm an encumbrance, when I should be helping. But they seem to be taking everything out of my hands.

Saturday the Second

I love to watch the wheat, now that it's really turning. It waves like a sea and stretches off into the distance as far as the eye can follow it. It's as high as my waist, and sometimes it moves up and down like a slowly breathing breast. When the sun is low it turns a pure Roman gold, and makes my eyes ache. But I love it. It strikes me as being glorious, and at the same time pathetic—I scarcely know why. I can't analyze my feelings. But the prairie brings a great peace to my soul. It is so rich, so maternal, so generous. It seems to brood under a passion to give, to yield up, to surrender all that is asked of it. And it is so tranquil. It seems like a bosom breathed on by the breath of God.

Wednesday the Sixth

It is nearly a year, now, since I first came to Casa Grande. I can scarcely believe it. The nights are getting very cool again and any time now there might be a heavy frost. If it should freeze this next week or two I think my Dinky-Dunk would just curl up and die. Poor boy, he's working so hard! I pray for that crop every night. I worry about it. Last night I dreamt it was burnt up in a prairie-fire and woke up screaming for wet blankets. Dinky-Dunk had to hold me until I got quiet again. I asked him if he loved me, now that I was getting old and ugly. He said I was the most beautiful thing God ever made and that he loved me in a deeper and nobler way than he did a year ago. Then I asked him if he'd ever get married again, if I should die. He called me silly and said I was going to live to be eighty, and that a gasoline-tractor couldn't kill me. But he promised I'd be the only one, whatever happened. And I believe him. I know Dinky-Dunk would go in black for a solid year, if I *should* die, and he'd never, never marry again, for he's the sort of Old Sobersides who can only love one woman in one lifetime. And I'm the woman, glory be!

Tuesday the Twelfth

Harvest time is here. The stage is cleared, and the last and great act of the drama now begins. It's a drama with a stage a thousand miles wide. I can hear through the open windows the rattle of the self-binders. Olga is driving one, like a tawny Boadicea up on her chariot. She said she never saw such heads of wheat. This is the first day's cutting, but those flapping canvas belts and those tireless arms of wood and iron won't have one-tenth of Dinky-Dunk's crop tied up by midnight. It is very cold, and Olie has lugubriously announced that it's sure going to freeze. So three times I've gone out to look at the thermometer and three times I've said my solemn little prayer: "Dear God, please don't freeze poor Dinky-Dunk's wheat!" And the Lord heard that prayer, for a Chinook came about two o'clock in the morning and the mercury slowly but steadily rose.

Thursday the Fourteenth

I had a great deal to talk about to-day. But I can't write much.... I'm afraid. I dread being alone. I wish I'd been a better wife to my poor old gold-bricked Dinky-Dunk! But we are what we are, character-kinks and all. So when he understands, perhaps he'll forgive me. I'm like a cottontail in the middle of a wheat-patch with the binders going round and round and every swathe cutting away a little more of my covering. And there can't be much more hiding away with my secret. But I shall never openly speak of it. The binder can cut off my feet first, the same as Olie's did with that mother-rabbit which stood trembling over her nest of young. Why must life sometimes be so ruthlessly tragic? And why, oh, why, are women sometimes so absurd? And why should I be afraid of what every woman who would justify her womanhood must face? Still, I'm afraid!

Wednesday the Fifth

Three long weeks since those last words were written. And what shall I say, or how shall I begin?

In the first place, everything seemed gray. The bed was gray, my own arms were gray, the walls looked gray, the window-glass was gray, and even Dinky-Dunk's face was gray. I didn't want to move, for a long time. Then I got the strength to tell Mrs. Watson that I wanted to speak to my husband. She was wrapping something up in soft flannel and purring over it quite proudly and calling it a blessed little lamb. When poor pale-faced Dinky-Dunk bent over the bed I asked him if it had a receding chin, or if it had a nose like Olie's. And he said it had neither, that it was a king of a boy and could holler like a good one.

Then I told Dinky-Dunk what had been in my secret soul, for so many months. Uncle Carlton had a receding chin, a boneless, dew-lappy sort of chin I'd always hated, and I'd been afraid it might kind of skip-and-carry one and fasten itself on my innocent offspring. Then, later on, I'd been afraid of Olie's frozen nose, with the split down the center. And all the while I kept remembering what the Morleys' old colored nurse had said to me when I was a schoolgirl, a girl of only seventeen, spending that first vacation of mine in Virginia: "Lawdy, chile, yuh ain't no bigger'n a minit! Don't yuh nebber hab no baby, chile!"

Isn't it funny how those foolish old things stick in a woman's memory? For I've had my baby and I'm still alive, and although I sometimes wanted a girl, Dinky-Dunk is so ridiculously proud and happy seeing it's a boy that I don't much care. But I'm going to get well and strong in a few more days, and here against my breast I'm holding the God-love-itest little lump of pulsing manhood, the darlingest, solemnest, placidest, pinkest hope of the white race that ever made life full and perfect for a foolish mother.

The doctor who finally got here—when both Olga and Mrs. Dixon agreed that he couldn't possibly do a bit of good—announced that I had come through it all like the true Prairie Woman that I was. Then he somewhat pompously and redundantly explained that I was a highly organized individual, "a bit high-strung," as Mrs. Dixon put it. I smiled into the pillow when he turned to my anxious-eyed Dinky-Dunk and condoningly enlarged on the fact that there was nothing abnormal about a woman like me being—well, rather abnormal as to temper and nerves during the last few months. But Dinky-Dunk cut him short.

"On the contrary, sir; she's been wonderful, simply wonderful!" Dinky-Dunk stoutly declared. Then he reached for my hand under the coverlet. "She's been an angel!"

I squeezed the hand that held mine. Then I looked at the doctor, who had turned away to give some orders to Olga.

"Doctor," I quite as stoutly declared, "I've been a perfect devil, and this dear old liar knows it!" But our doctor was too busy to pay much attention to what I was saying. He merely murmured that it was all normal, quite normal, under the circumstances. So, after all, I'm just an ordinary, everyday woman! But the man of medicine has ordered me to stay in bed for twelve days—which Olga regards as unspeakably preposterous, since one day, she proudly announced, was all her mother ever asked for. Which shows the disadvantages of being too civilized!

Sunday the Ninth

I'm day by day getting stronger, though I'm a lady of luxury and lie in bed until ten every morning. To-day when I was sitting up to eat breakfast, with my hair braided in two tails and a pink and white hug-me-tight over my nightie, Dinky-Dunk came in and sat by the bed. He tried to soft-soap me by saying he'd be mighty glad when I was running things again so he could get something fit to eat. Olga, he admitted, was all right, but she hadn't the touch of his Gee-Gee. He confessed that for nearly a month now the house had been a damned gynocracy and he was getting tired of being bossed around by a couple of women. *Mio piccino* no longer looks like a littered whelp of the animal world, as he did at first. His wrinkled little face and his close-shut eyes used to make me think of a little old man, with all the wisdom of the ages shut up in his tiny body. And it is such a knowing little body, with all its stored-up instincts and guardian appetites! My little *tenor robusto*, how he can sing when he's hungry! Last night I sat up in bed, listening for my son's—Dinky-Dink's—breathing. At first I thought he might be dead, he was so quiet. Then I heard his lips move in the rhapsodic deglutition of babyland dreams. "Dinky-Dunk," I demanded, "what would we do if Babe should die?" And I shook him to make him answer. He stared up at me with a sleepy eye. "That whale?" he commented as he blinked contentedly down at his offspring and then turned over and went to sleep. But I slipped a hand in under little Dinky-Dink's body, and found it as warm as a nesting bird.

Monday the Tenth

I noticed that Dinky-Dunk had not been smoking lately, so I asked him what had become of the rest of his cigars. He admitted that he had given them to Olie. "When?" I asked. And Dinky-Dunk colored up as he answered, rather casually, "Oh, the day Buddy Boy was born!" How men merge down into the conventional in their more epochal moments!

The second day after my baby's birth Olga rather took my breath away by carrying in as neat a little wooden cradle as any prince of the royal blood would care to lie in. *Olie had made it*. He had worked on it during his spare hours in the evening, and even Dinky-Dunk hadn't known. I made Olga hold it up at the foot of the bed so I could see it better. It had been scroll-sawed and sand-papered and polished like any factory-made baby-bed, and my faithful old Olie had even attempted some hand-carving along the rockers and the head-board. But as I looked at it I realized that it must have taken weeks and weeks to make. And that gave me an odd little earthquaky feeling in the neighborhood of the midriff, for I knew then that my secret had been no secret at all. Dinky-Dunk, by the way, has just announced that we're to have a touring-car. He says I've earned it!

Tuesday the Eleventh

Yesterday was so warm that I sat out in the sun and took an ozone-bath. I sat there, staring down at my boy, realizing that I was a mother. My boy—bone of my bone and flesh of my flesh! It's so hard to believe! And now I am one of the mystic chain, and no longer the idle link. I am a mother. And I'd give an arm if you and Chinkie and Scheming-Jack could see my boy, at this moment. He's like a rose-leaf and he's got six dimples, not counting his hands and feet—for I've found and kissed 'em all—on different parts of his blessed little body. Dinky-Dunk came back from Buckhorn yesterday with a lot of the foolishest things you ever clapped eyes on—a big cloth elephant that grunts when you pull its tail, a musical spinning-top, a high-chair, and a projecting lantern. They're for Dinky-Dink, of course. But it will be a week or two before he can manipulate the lantern!

Wednesday the Thirteenth

Dinky-Dunk has taken Mrs. Dixon home and come back with a brand-new "hand," which, of course, is prairie-land synecdoche for a new hired man. His name is Terry Dillon, and as the name might lead you to imagine, he's about as Irish as Paddy's pig. He is blessed with a potato-lip, a buttermilk brogue, and a nose which, if he follows it faithfully, will some day lead him straight to Heaven. But Terry, Dinky-Dunk tells me, is a steady worker and a good man with horses, and that of course rounds him out as a paragon in the eyes of my slave-driving lord and master. I asked where Terry came from. Dinky-Dunk, with rather a grim smile, acknowledged that he'd been working for Percy.

Terry, it seems, has no particular love for an Englishman. And Percy had affronted his haughty Irish spirit with certain ideas of caste which can't be imported into the Canadian West, where the hired man is every whit as good as his master—as that master will tragically soon find out if he tries to make his help eat at second table! At any rate, Percy and potato-lipped Terry developed friction which ended up in every promise of a fight, only Dinky-Dunk arrived in the nick of time and took Terry off his harassed neighbor's hands. I told him he had rather the habit of catching people on the bounce. But I am reserving my opinion of Terry Dillon. We are a happy family here, and I want no trouble-makers in my neighborhood.

I have been studying some of the New York magazines, going rather hungrily through their advertisements where such lovely layettes are described. My poor little Dinky-Dink's things are so plain and rough and meager. I envy those city mothers with all those beautiful linens and laces. But my little Spartan man-child has never known a single day's sickness. And some day he'll show 'em!

Thursday the Fourteenth

When Olie came in after dinner yesterday I asked him where my husband was. Olie, after some hesitation, admitted that he was out in the stable. I asked just what Dinky-Dunk was doing there, for I'd noticed that after each meal he slipped silently away. Again Olie hesitated. Then he finally admitted that he thought maybe my lord was out there smoking. So I went out, and there I found my poor old Dinky-Dunk sitting on a grain-box puffing gloomily away at his old pipe. For a minute or two he didn't see me, so I went right over to him. "What does this mean?" I demanded.

"Why?" he rather guiltily equivocated.

"Why are you smoking out here?"

"I—er—I rather thought you might think it wouldn't be good for the Boy!" He looked pathetic as he said that, I don't know why, though I loved him for it. He made me think of a king who'd been dethroned, an outsider, a man without a home. It brought a lump into my throat.

I wormed my way up close to him on the grain-box, so that he had to hold me to keep from falling off the end. "Listen to me," I commanded. "You are my True Love and my Kaikobád and my Man-God and my Soul-Mate! And no baby is ever going to come between me and you!"

"You shouldn't say those awful things," he declared, but he did it only half-heartedly.

"But I want you to sit and smoke with me, beloved, the same as you always did," I told him. "We can leave the windows open a little and it won't hurt Dinky-Dink, for that boy gets more ozone than any city child that was ever wheeled out in the Mall! It can't possibly hurt him. What hurts me is being away from you so much. And now give me a hug, a tight one, and tell me that you still love your Lady Bird!" He gave me two, and then two more, until Tumble-Weed turned round in his stall and whinnied for us to behave.

Friday the Fifteenth

I've been keeping Terry under my eye, and I don't believe he's a trouble-maker. His first move was to lift Babe out of the cradle, hold him up and publicly announce that he was a darlin'. Then he pointed out to me what a wonderful head the child had, feeling his frontal bone and declaring he was sure to make a great scholar in his time. Dinky-Dunk, grinning at the sober way in which I was swallowing this, pointedly inquired of Terry whether it was Milton or Archimedes that Babe most resembled as to skull formation. But it isn't Terry's blarney that has made me capitulate; it's the fact that he has proved so companionable and has slipped so quietly into his place in our little lonely circle of lives on this ragged edge of nowhere.

And he's as clean as a cat, shaving every blessed morning with a little old broken-handled razor which he strops on a strip of oiled bootleg. He declares that razor to be the finest bit of steel in all the Americas, and showed off before Olie and Olga yesterday morning by shaving without a looking-glass, which trick he said he learned in the army. He also gave Olie a hair-cut, which was badly needed, and on Sunday has promised to rig up a soldering-iron and mend all my pans for me. He looks little over twenty, but is really thirty and more, and has been in India and Mexico and Alaska.

I caught him neatly darning his own woolen socks. Instead of betraying shame at being detected in that effeminate pastime he proudly explained that he'd learned to do a bit of stitching in the army. He hasn't many possessions, but he's very neat in his arrangement of them. A good soldier, he solemnly told me, always had to be a bit of an old maid. "And you were a grand soldier, Terry, I know," I frankly told him. "I've done a bit av killing in me time!" he proudly acknowledged. But as he sat there darning his sock-heel he looked as though he couldn't kill a field mouse. And in his idle hours he reads *Nick Carter*, a series of paper-bound detective stories, almost worn to tatters, which he is going through for the second or third time. These adventures, I find, he later recounts to Olie, who is slowly but surely succumbing to the poison of the penny-dreadful and the virus of the shilling-shocker! I even caught Dinky-Dunk sitting up over one of these blood-curdling romances the other night, though he laughed a little as I dragged him off to bed, at the absurdity of the situations. Terry's eyes lighted up when he saw my books and magazines. When I told him he could take anything he wanted, he beamed and said it would sure be a glorious winter he'd be having, with all that book-reading when the long nights came. But before those long nights are over I'm going to try to pilot Terry into the channels of respectable literature.

Saturday the Sixteenth

I love the milky smell of my Dinky-Dink better than the perfume of any flower that ever grew. He's so strong now that he can almost lift himself up by his two little hands. At least he can really and actually give a little *pull*. Two days ago our touring-car arrived. It is a beauty. It skims over these smooth prairie trails like a yacht. From now on we can run into Buckhorn, do our shopping, and run out again inside of two or three hours. We can also reach the larger towns without trouble and it will be so much easier to gather up what we need for Casa Grande. Dinky-Dink seems to love the car. Ten minutes after we have started out he is always fast asleep. Olga, who holds him in the back seat when I get tired, sits in rapt and silent bliss as we rock along at thirty miles an hour. And no wonder, for it's the next best thing to sailing out on the briny deep!

I can't help thinking of Terry's attitude toward Olga. He doesn't actively dislike her, but he quietly ignores her, even more so than Olie does. I've been wondering why neither of them has succumbed to such physical grandeur. Perhaps it's because they're physical themselves. And then I think her largeness oppresses Terry, for no man, whether he's been a soldier or not, likes to be overtopped by a woman.

The one exception, of course, is Percy. But Percy is a man of imagination. He can realize that Olga is more than a mere type. He agrees with me that she's a sort of miracle. To Terry she's only a mute and muscular Finnish servant-girl with an arm like a grenadier's. To Percy she is a goddess made manifest, a superhuman body of superhuman vigor and beauty and at the same time a body crowned with majesty and robed in mystery. And I still incline to Percy's opinion. Olga is always wonderful to me. Her lips are such a soft and melting red, the red of perfect animal health. The very milkiness of her skin is an advertisement of that queenly and all-conquering vitality which lifts her so above the ordinary ruck of humanity. And her great ruminative eyes are as clear and limpid as any woodland pool.

She blushes rose color sometimes when Percy comes in. I think he finds a secret joy in sensing that reaction in anything so colossal. But he defends himself behind that mask of cool impersonality which is the last attribute of the mental aristocrat, no matter what his feelings may be. His attitude toward Terry, by the way, is a remarkably companionable one in view of the fact of their earlier contentions. They can let by-gones be by-gones and talk and smoke and laugh together. It is Terry, if any one, who is just a wee bit condescending. And I imagine that it is the aura of Olga which has brought about this oddly democratizing condition of affairs. She seems to give a new relationship to things, softening a point here and illuminating a point there as quietly as moonlight itself can do.

Monday the Seventeenth

Yesterday Olga carried home a whole pailful of mushrooms, for an Indian summer seems to have brought on a second crop of them. They were lovely. But she refused to eat any. I asked her why. She heaved her huge shoulders and said she didn't know. But she does, I feel sure, and I've been wondering why she's afraid of anything that can taste so good, once they are creamed and heaped on a square of toast. As for me

I love 'em, I love 'em, and who shall dareTo chide me for loving that mushroom fare?

Wednesday the Nineteenth

I found myself singing for all I was worth as I did my work this morning. Dinky-Dunk came and stood in the door and said it sounded like old times. I feel strong again and have ventured to ask my lord and master if I couldn't have the weentiest gallop on Paddy once more. But he's made me promise to wait for a week or two. The last two or three nights have been quite cold, and away off, miles and miles across the prairie, we can see the glow of fires where different ranchers are burning their straw, after the wind-stackers have blown it from the threshing machines. Sometimes it burns all night long.

Friday the Twenty-first

I have this morning found out why Olga won't eat mushrooms. It was very cold again last night, for this time of year. Percy came over, and we had a ripping fire and popped Ontario pop-corn with Ontario maple sirup poured over it. Olga and Olie and Terry all came in and sat about the stove. And being absolutely happy and contented and satisfied with life in general, we promptly fell to talking horrors, the same as a cook stirs lemon juice into her pudding-sauce, I suppose, to keep its sweetness from being too cloying. That revel in the by-paths of the Poesque began with Dinky-Dunk's casual reference to the McKinnon ranch and Percy's inquiry as to why its earlier owner had given it up. So Dinky-Dunk recounted the story of Andrew Cochrane's death. And it was noticeable that poor old Olie betrayed visible signs of distress at this tale of a young ranchman being frozen to death alone in his shack in mid-winter. So Dinky-Dunk, apparently with malice prepense, enlarged on his theme, describing how all young Cochrane's stock had starved in their stalls and how his collie dog which had been chained to a kennel-box outside the shack had first drawn attention to the tragedy. A government inspector, in riding past, had noticed the shut-up shack, had pounded on the door, and had promptly discovered the skeleton of the dog with a chain and collar still attached to the clean-picked neckbones. And inside the shack he had found the dead man himself, as life-like, because of the intense cold, as though he had fallen asleep the night before.

It was not a pleasant story, and my efforts to picture the scene gave me rather a bristly feeling along the pin-feather area of my anatomy. And again undoubted signs of distress were manifest in poor Olie. The face of that simple-souled Swede took on such a look of wondering trouble that Dinky-Dunk deliberately and at great detail told of a ghost that had been repeatedly seen in an abandoned wickyup a little farther west in the province.

And that, of course, fired the Celtic soul of Terry, who told of the sister of his Ould Counthry master who had once been taken to a hospital. And just at dusk on the third day after that his young master was walking down the dark hall. As he passed his sister's door, there she stood all in white, quietly brushing her hair, as plain as day to his eyes. And with that the master rushed down-stairs to his mother asking how Sheila had got back from the hospital. And his old mother, being slow of movement, started for Sheila's room. But before she so much as reached the foot of the stairs a neighbor woman came running in, wiping her eyes with her shawl-end and saying,

"Poor Sheila died this minute over t' the hospital!" I can't tell it as Terry told it, and I don't know whether he himself believed in it or not, but the huge bulk of Olie Larson sat there bathed in a fine sweat, with his eyes fixed on the stove front. He was by no means happy, and yet he seemed unable to tear himself away, just as Gimlets and I used to sit chained to the spot while Grandfather Heppelwhite continued to intone the dolorous history of the "Babes in the Woods" until our ultimate and inevitable collapse into tears!

So Percy, who is not without his spirit of ragging, told several whoppers, which he later confessed came from the Society of Psychical Research records. And I huskily recounted Uncle Carlton's story of the neurasthenic lady patient who went into a doctor's office and there beheld a skull standing on his polished rosewood desk. Then, as she sat staring at it, this skull started to move slowly toward her. It later turned out to be only a plaster-of-Paris paper weight, and a mouse had got inside it and found a piece of cracker there—and a cracker, I had to explain to Percy, was the name under which a biscuit usually masqueraded in America. That mouse, in its efforts to get the last of that cracker, had, of course, shifted the skull along the polished wood.

This reminded Dinky-Dunk of the three medical students who had tried to frighten their landlady's daughter by smuggling an arm from the dissecting room and hiding it under the girl's pillow. Dinky-Dunk even solemnly avowed that the three men were college chums of his. They waited to hear the girl's scream, but as there was nothing but silence they finally stole into the room. And there they saw the girl sitting on the floor, holding the arm in her hands. As she sat there she was mumbling to herself and eating one end of it! Of course the poor thing had gone stark staring mad.

Olie groaned audibly at this and wiped his forehead with his coat-sleeve. But before he could get away Terry started to tell of the four-bottle Irish sea captain who was sober only when at sea and one night in port stumbled up to bed three sheets in the wind. When he had navigated into what he thought was his own room he was astounded to find a man already in bed there, and even drunker than he was himself, too drunk, in fact, to move. And even the candles had been left burning. But the old captain climbed over next to the wall, clothes and all, and would have been fast asleep in two minutes if two stout old ladies hadn't come in and started to cry and say a prayer or two at the side of the bed. Thereupon the old captain, muddled as he was, quietly but inquisitively reached over and touched the man beside him. *And that man was cold as ice!* The captain gave one howl and made for the door. But the old ladies went first, and they all rolled down the stairs one after the other and the three of them up and ran like the wind. "And niver wanst did they stop," declared the brogue-mouthing Terry, "till they lept flat against the sea-wall!"

Olie, who had moved away to the far end of the table, got up at this point and went to the door and looked out. He sighed lugubriously as he stared into the darkness of the night. The outer gloom, apparently, was too much for him, as he came slowly and reluctantly back to his chair at the far end of the table and it was plain to see that he was as frightened as a five-year-old child. The men, I suppose, would have badgered him until midnight, for Terry had begun a story of a negro who'd been sent to rob a grave and found the dead man not quite dead. But I declared that we'd had enough of horrors and declined to hear anything more about either ghosts or deaders. I was, in fact, getting just a wee bit creepy along the nerve-ends myself. And Babe whimpered a little in his cradle and brought us all suddenly back from the Wendigo Age to the time of the kerosene lamp. "Fra' witches and warlocks," I solemnly intoned, "fra' wurricoos and evil speerits, and fra' a' ferly things that wheep and gang bump in the nicht, Guid Lord deliver us!" And that incantation, I feel sure, cleared the air for both my own sprite-threatened offspring and for the simple-minded Olie himself, although Dinky-Dunk explained that my Scotch was rather worse than the stories.

But it was this morning after breakfast that I learned from Olga why she never cared to eat mushrooms. And all day long her story has been hanging between me and the sun, like a cloud. Not that there is anything so wonderful about the story itself, outside of its naked tragedy. But I think it was more the way that huge placid-eyed girl told it, with her broken English and her occasional pauses to grope after the right word. Or perhaps it was because it came as such a grim reality after the trifling grotesqueries of the night before. At any rate, as I heard it this morning it seemed as terrible as anything in Tolstoi's *Heart of Darkness*, and more than once sent my thoughts back to the sorrows of the house of Œdipus. It startled me a little, too, for I never thought to catch an echo of Greek tragedy out of the full soft lips of a Finnish girl who was helping me wash my breakfast dishes.

It began as I was deciding on my dinner menu, and looked to see if all our mushrooms had been used up. That prompted me to ask the girl why she never ate them. I could see a barricaded look come into her eyes but she merely shrugged and said that sometimes they were poison and killed people. I told her that this was absurd and that any one with ordinary intelligence soon got to know a meadow mushroom when he saw one. But sometimes, Olga insisted, they were death cups. If you ate a death cup you died, and nothing could save you. I tried to convince her that this was just a peasant superstition, but she announced that she had seen death cups, many of them, and had seen people who had been killed by them. And then brokenly, and with many heavy gestures of hesitation, she told me the story.

Nearly seventy miles northwest of us, up near her old home, so she said, a Pole named Andrei Przenikowski and his wife used to live. They had one son, whose name was Jozef. They were poor, always poor, and could never succeed. So when Jozef was fifteen years old he went to the coast to make his fortune. And the old father and mother had a hard time of it, for old Andrei found it no easy thing to get about, having had his feet frozen years before. He stumped around like a hen with frost-bitten claws, Olga said, and his wife, old as she was, had to help him in the fields. One whole winter, he told Olga's father, they had lived on turnips. But season after season dragged on, and still they existed, God knows how. Of Jozef they never heard again. But with Jozef himself it was a different story. The boy went up to Alaska, before the days of the Klondike strike. There he worked in the fisheries, and in the lumber camps, and still later he joined a mining outfit. Then he went in to the Yukon.

That was twelve years after he had first left home. He was a strong man by this time and spoke English very well. And the next year he struck luck, and washed up a great deal of gold, thousands of dollars' worth of gold. But he saved it all, for he had never forgotten the old folks on their little farm. So he gathered up his money and went down to Seattle, and then crossed to Vancouver. From there he made his way back to his old home, dressed like a man of the world and wearing a big gold watch and chain and a gold ring. And when he walked in on the old folks they failed to recognize him—and that Jozef thought the finest of jokes. He filled the little sod-covered shack with his laughter, for he was happy. He knew that for the rest of their days their troubles had all ended. So he walked about and made plans, but still he did not tell them who he was. It was so good a joke that he intended to make the most of it. But he said that he had news of their Jozef, who was not so badly off for a ne'er-do-well. Before he left the next day, he promised, they should be told about their boy. And he laughed again and slapped his pocketful of gold and the two old folks sat blinking at him in awe, until he announced that he was hungry and confided to them that his friend Jozef had once told him there were wonderful mushrooms roundabout at that season of the year.

Andrei and his wife talked together in the cow-shed, before the old man hobbled out to gather the mushrooms. Poverty and suffering had made them hard and the sight of this stranger with so much gold was too much for them. So it was a plate full of death cups which Andrei's wife cooked for the brown-faced stranger with the loud laugh. And they stood about and watched him eat them. Then he died, as Andrei knew he must die. But the old woman hid in the cow-shed until it was over, for it took some time. Together then the old couple searched the dead man's bags and his pockets. They found papers and certain marks on his body. They knew then that they had murdered their own son. The old man hobbled all the way to the nearest village, where he sent a letter to Olga's father and bought a clothes-line to take home. The journey took him an entire day. With that clothes-line Andrei Przenikowski and his wife hanged themselves, from one of the rafters in the cow-shed.

Olga said that she was only five years old then, but she remembered driving over with the others, after the letter had come to her father's place. She can still remember seeing the two old bodies hanging side by side and twisting slowly about in the wind. And she saw what was left of the mushrooms. She says she can never forget it and dreams of it quite often. And Olga is not what you would call emotional. She told me, as she dried her hands and hung up the dish-pan, that she can still see her people staring down at what was left of that plate of poisoned death cups, which had turned quite black, almost as black as the dead man she saw them lift up on the dirty bed.

Monday the Twelfth

Yesterday was Sunday and Olga in her best bib and tucker sat out in the sun with Dinky-Dink. She seemed perfectly happy merely to hold him. I looked out, to make sure he was all right, for a few days before Olga had nearly given me heart failure by balancing my boy on one huge hand, as though he were a mutton-chop, so that the adoring Olie might see him kick. As I stood watching Olga crooning above Buddy Boy, Percy rode up. Then he came over and joined Olga, who carefully lifted up the veil covering Dinky-Dink's face, and showed him off to the somewhat intimidated Percy. Percy poked a finger at him, and made absurd noises, and felt his legs as Olga directed and then sat down in front of Olga.

They talked there for a long time, quite oblivious of everything about them. At least Percy talked, for Olga's replies seemed mostly monosyllabic. But she kept bathing him in that mystic moonlight stare of hers and sometimes she showed her teeth in a slow and wistful sort of smile. Percy clattered on, quite unconscious that I was standing in the doorway staring at him. They seemed to be great pals. And I've been wondering what they talked about.

Wednesday the Fourteenth

To-day after dinner Dinky-Dunk took the Boy and held him up on Paddy's back, where he looked like a bump on a log. And that started me thinking that it wouldn't be so long before my little Snoozerette had a pony of his own and would be cantering off across the prairie like a monkey on a circus horse. For I want my boy to ride, and ride well. And then a little later he would be cantering off to school. And then it wouldn't be such a great while before he'd be hitting the trail side by side with some clear-eyed prairie girl on a dappled pinto, and I'd be a silvery-haired old lady wondering if that clear-eyed girl was good enough for my son! And there I was, as usual, dreaming of the future!

All day long the fact that Dinky-Dunk is getting extravagant has been hitting me just under the fifth rib. So I asked him if we could really afford a six-cylinder car with tan slip-covers and electric lights. "Afford it?" he echoed, "of course we can afford it. We can afford anything. Hang it all, our lean days are over and we haven't had the imagination to wake up to the fact. And d'you know what I'm going to do if certain things come my way? I'm going to send you and the Babe down to New York for the winter!"

"And where will you be?" I promptly inquired. The look of mingled pride and determination went out of his face.

"Oh, I'll have to hang around the Polar regions up here to look after things. But you and the Boy have got to have your chance. And I'll come down for two weeks at Easter and bring you home with me!"

"And will you be enjoying it up here?" I inquired.

"Of course I won't," acknowledged Dinky-Dunk. "But think what it will mean to you, Gee-Gee, to have a few months in the city again! And think what you've been missing!"

"Goosey-goosey-gander!" I said as I got his foolish old head in Chancery. "I want you to listen to me. There's nothing I've been missing. And you are plum locoed, Honey Chile, if you think I could ever be happy away from you, in New York or any other city. And I wouldn't go there for the winter if you gave me the Plaza and all the Park for a back yard!"

That declaration of mine seemed to puzzle him. "But think what it would mean to the Boy!" he contended.

"Well, what?" I demanded.

"Oh, good—er—good pictures and music and all that sort of thing!" he vaguely explained. I couldn't help laughing at him.

"But, Dinky-Dunk, don't you think Babe's a month or so too young to take up Debussy and the Post-Impressionists, you big, foolish, adorable old muddle-headed captor of helpless ladies' hearts!" And I firmly announced that he could never, never get rid of me.

Thursday the Fifteenth

Now that Olga is working altogether inside with me she is losing quite a little of her sunburn. Her skin is softer and she has acquired a little more of the Leonardo di Vinci look. She almost seems to be getting spiritualized—but it may be simply because she's lengthened her skirts. She loves Babe, and, I'm afraid, is rather spoiling him. I find her a better and better companion, not only because she talks more, but because she seems in some way to be climbing up to a newer level. Between whiles, I'm teaching her to cook. She learns readily, and is proud of her progress. But the thing of which she is proudest is her corsets. And they *do* make a difference. Even Dinky-Dunk has noticed this. Yesterday he stood and stared after her.

"By gum," he sagely remarked, "that girl is getting a figure!" Men are so absurd. When this same Olga was going about half uncovered he never even noticed her. Now that she's mystified her nether limbs with a little drapery he stands staring after her as though she were a Venus de Milo come to life. And Olga is slowly but surely losing a little of her Arcadian simplicity. Yesterday I caught her burning up her cowhide boots. She is ashamed of them. And she is spending most of her money on clothes, asking me many strange questions as to apparel and carrying off my fashion magazines to her bedroom for secret perusal. For the first time in her life she is using cold cream. And the end seems to justify the means, for her skin is now like apple blossoms. Rodin, I feel sure, would have carried that woman across America on his back, once to have got her into his atelier!

Last week I persuaded Terry to take a try at Meredith and lent him my green cloth copy of *Harry Richmond*. Three days ago I found the seventh page turned down at the corner, and suspecting that this marked the final frontier of his advance, I tied a strand of green silk thread about the volume. It was still there this morning, though Terry daily and stoutly maintains that he's getting on grand with that fine green book of mine! But at noon to-day when Dinky-Dunk got back from Buckhorn he handed Terry a parcel, and I noticed the latter glanced rather uneasily about as he unwrapped it. This afternoon I discovered that it held two new books in paper covers. One was *The Hidden Hand* and the other was called *The Terror of Tamaraska Gulch*. Terry, of late, has been doing his reading in his own room. And Nick Carter, apparently, is not to be so easily displaced. But a man who can make you read his books for the third time must be a genius. If I were an author, that's the sort of man I'd envy. And I think I'll try

Percival Benson with *The Terror of Tamaraska Gulch* when Terry is through with it!

Friday the Sixteenth

We were just finishing dinner to-day, and an uncommonly good one it seemed to me, and I was looking contentedly about my little family circle, wondering what more life could hold for a big healthy hulk of a woman like me, when the drone and purr of an approaching motor-car broke through the sound of our talk. Dinky-Dunk, in fact, was laying down the law about the farmer of the West, maintaining that he was a broader-spirited and bigger-minded man than his brother of the East, and pointing out that the westerner's wife was a queen who if she had little ease at least had great honor. And I was just thinking that one glorious thing about this same queen was that she at least escaped from all the twentieth-century strain and dislocation in the relationship between city men and women, when the hum of that car brought me back to earth and reminded me that I might have a tableful of guests to feed. The car itself drew up, with a flutter of its engine, half-way between the shack and the corral, and at that sound I imagine we all rather felt like Robinson Crusoes listening to the rattle of an anchor cable in Juan Fernandez's quietest bay. And through the open window I could make out a huge touring-car pretty well powdered with dust and with no less than six men in it.

Terry, all eyes, dove for the window, and Olie, all mouth, for the door. Olga leaned half-way across the table to look out, and I did a little staring myself. The only person who remained quiet was Dinky-Dunk. He knocked out his pipe, stuck it in his pocket, put on his hat and caught up a package of papers from his work table. Then he stalked out, with his gray fighting look about the eyes. He went out just as one of the bigger men was about to step down from the car, so that the bigger man changed his mind and climbed back in his seat, like a king reascending his throne. And they all sat there so sedate and non-committal and dignified, rather like dusty pallbearers in an undertaker's wagonette, that I promptly decided they had come to foreclose a mortgage and take my Dinky-Dunk's land away from him, at one fell swoop!

I could see my lord walk right up to the running-board, with curt little nods to his visitors, and I knew by the trim of his shoulders that there was trouble ahead. Yet they started talking quietly enough. But inside of two minutes my Dinky-Dunk was shaking his fist in the face of one of the younger and bigger men and calling him a liar and somewhat tautologically accusing him of knowing that he was a liar and that he always had been one. This altogether ungentlemanly language naturally brought forth language quite as ungentlemanly from the accused, who stood up in the car and took his turn at dancing about and shaking his own fist. And then the others seemed to take sides, and voices rose to a shout, and I saw that there was going to be another fight at Casa Grande—and I promptly decided to be in it. So off went my apron and out I went.

It was funny. For, oddly enough, the effect of my entrance on the scene was like that on a noisy class-room at the teacher's return. The tumult stopped, rather sheepishly, and that earful of men instinctively slipped on their armor plate of over-obsequious sex gallantry. They knew I wasn't a low-brow. I went right up to them, though something about their funereal discomfiture made me smile. So Dinky-Dunk, mad as a wet hen though he was, had to introduce every man-jack of them to me! One was a member of Parliament, and another belonged to some kind of railway committee, and another was a road construction official, and another was a mere capitalist who owned two or three newspapers. The man Dinky-Dunk had been calling a liar was a civil engineer, although it seemed to me that he had been acting decidedly uncivil. They ventured a platitude about the beautiful Indian summer weather and labored out a ponderous joke or two about such a bad-tempered man having such a good-looking wife—for which I despised them all. But I could see that even if my intrusion had put the soft pedal on their talk it had also left everything uncomfortably tentative and non-committal. For some reason or other this was a man's fight, one which had to be settled in a man's way. So I decided to retire with outward dignity even if with inward embarrassment. But I resented their uncouth commercial gallantry almost as much as I abominated their trying to bully my True Love. And I gave them one Parthian shot as I turned away.

"The last prize-fight I saw was in a sort of *souteneur's* cabaret in the Avenue des Tilleuls," I sweetly explained to them. "But that was nearly three years ago. So if there is going to be a bout in my back yard, I trust you gentlemen will be so good as to call me!"

And smiling up into their somewhat puzzled faces, I turned on my heel and went into the house. One of the men laughed loud and deep, at this speech of mine, and a couple of the others seemed to sit puzzling over it. Yet two minutes after I was inside the shack that most uncivil civil engineer and Dinky-Dunk were at it again. Their language was more than I should care to repeat. The end of it was, however, that the six dusty pallbearers all stepped stiffly down out of their car and Dinky-Dunk shouted for Olie and Terry. At first I thought it was to be a duel, only I couldn't make out how it could be fought with a post-hole augur and a few lengths of jointed gaspipe, for this was what the men carried away with them.

Away across the prairie I could see them apparently engaged in the silly and quite profitless occupation of putting down a post-hole where it wasn't in the least needed, and then clustering about this hole like a bunch of professorial bigwigs about a new specimen on a microscope slide. Then they moved on and made another hole, and still another, until I got tired of watching them. It was two hours later before they came back. Their voices now seemed more facetious and there was more laughing and joking, Dinky-Dunk and the uncivil civil engineer being the only quiet ones. And then the car engine purred and hummed and they climbed heavily in and lighted cigars and waved hands and were off in a cloud of dust.

But Dinky-Dunk, when he came back to the shack with his papers, was in no mood for talking. And I knew better than to try to pump him. To-night he came in early for supper and announced that he'd have to leave for Winnipeg right away and might even have to go on to Ottawa. So I cooked his supper and packed his bag and held Babe up for him to kiss good-by. But still I didn't bother him with questions, for I was afraid of bad news. And he knew that I knew I could trust him.

He kissed me good-by in a tragically tender, or rather a tenderly tragic sort of way, which made me wonder for a moment if he was possibly never coming back again. So I made 'em all wait while I took one extra, for good measure, in case I should be a grass widow for the rest of my days.

To-night, however, I sat Terry down at the end of the table and third degreed him to the queen's taste. The fight, as far as I can learn from this circuitous young Irishman, is all about a right of way through our part of the province. Dinky-Dunk, it seems, has been working for it for over a year. And the man he called wicked names had been sent out by the officials to report on the territory. My husband claims he was bribed by the opposition party and turned in a report saying our district was without water. He also proclaimed that our land—*our* land, mark you!—was unvaryingly poor and inferior soil! No wonder my Dinky-Dunk had stormed! Then Terry rather disquieted me by chortlingly announcing that they had put one over on the whole bunch. For, three days before, he'd quietly put down twenty soil and water-test holes and carefully filled them in again. But he'd found what he was after. And that little army of paid knockers, he acknowledged, had been steered into the neighborhood where the soil was deepest and the water was nearest. And that soon showed who the liar was, for of course everything came out as Dinky-Dunk wanted it to come out!

But this phase of it I didn't discuss with Terry, for I had no desire to air my husband's moral obliquities before his hired man. Yet I am still disturbed by what I have heard. Oh, Dinky-Dunk, I never imagined you were one bit sly, even in business!

Sunday the Eighteenth

Olie and Terry seem convinced of the fact that Dinky-Dunk's farming has been a success. We have saved all our wheat crop, and it's a whopper. Terry, with his crazy Celtic enthusiasms, says that by next year they'll be calling Dinky-Dunk the Wheat King of the West. Olga and Percy went buggy riding this afternoon. I wish I had some sort of scales to weight my Snoozerette. I know he's doubled in the last three weeks.

Sunday the Twenty-fifth

My Dinky-Dunk is home again. He looks a little tired and hollow-eyed, but when the Boy crowed and smiled up at him his poor tired face softened so wonderfully that it brought the tears to my eyes. I finally persuaded him to stop petting Babe and pay a little attention to me. After supper he opened up his extra hand-bag and hauled out the heaps of things he'd brought Babe and me. Then I sat on his knee and held his ears and made him blow away the smoke, every shred of it, so I could kiss him in my own particular places.

Tuesday the Twenty-seventh

Dinky-Dunk has sailed off to Buckhorn to do some telegraphing he should have done Saturday night. My suspicions about his slyness, by the way, were quite unfounded. It was the guileless-eyed Terry who led those railway officials out to the spot where he'd already secretly tested for water and found signs of it. And Terry can't even understand why Dinky-Dunk is so toweringly angry about it all!

Wednesday the Twenty-eighth

When Dinky-Dunk came in last night, after his drive out from Buckhorn, there was a look on his face that rather frightened me. I backed him up against the door, after he'd had a peep at the Boy, and said, "Let me smell your breath, sir!" For with that strange light in his eyes I surely thought he'd been drinking. "Lips that touch liquor," I sang, "shall never touch mine!"

But I was mistaken. And Dinky-Dunk only laughed in a quiet inward rumbling sort of way that was new to him. "I believe I am drunk, Boca Chica," he solemnly confessed, "drunk as a lord!" Then he took both my hands in his.

"D'you know what's going to happen?" he demanded. And of course I didn't. Then he hurled it point-blank at me.

"*The railway's going to come!*"

"Come where?" I gasped.

"Come here, right across our land! It's settled. And there's no mistake about it this time. Inside of ten months there'll be choo-choo cars steaming past Casa Grande!"

"Skookum!" I shouted.

"And there'll be a station within a mile of where you stand! And inside of two years this seventeen or eighteen hundred acres of land will be worth forty dollars an acre, easily, and perhaps even fifty. And what that means you can figure out for yourself!"

"Whoopee!" I gasped, trying in vain to figure out how much forty times seventeen hundred was.

But that was not all. It would do away with the road haul to the elevator, which might have taken most of the profit out of his grain growing. To team wheat into Buckhorn would have been a terrible discount, no matter what luck he might have with his crops. So he'd been moving heaven and earth to get the steel to come his way. He'd pulled wires and interviewed members and guaranteed a water-tank supply and promised a right of way and made use of his old engineering friends—until his battle was won. And his last fight had been against the liar who'd sent in false reports about his district. But that was over now, and Casa Grande will no longer be the jumping-off place of civilization, the dot on the wilderness. It will be on the time-tables and the mail-routes, and I know my Dinky-Dunk will be the first mayor of the new city, if there ever is a city to be mayor of!

Friday the Thirtieth

Dinky-Dunk came in at noon to-day, tiptoed over to the crib to see if the Boy was all right, and then came and put his hands on my shoulders, looking me solemnly in the eye: "What do you suppose has happened?" he demanded.

"Another railroad," I ventured.

He shook his head. Of course it was useless for me to try to guess. I pushed my finger against Dinky-Dunk's Adam's apple and asked him what the news was.

"Percival Benson Woodhouse has just calmly announced to me that, next week, *he's going to marry Olga*," was my husband's answer.

And he wondered why I smiled.

Sunday the First

Little Dinky-Dink is fast asleep in his hand-carved Scandinavian cradle. The night is cool, so we have a fire going. Big Dinky-Dunk, who has been smoking his pipe, is sitting on one side of the table, and I am sitting on the other. Between us lies the bundle of house-plans which have just been mailed up to us from Philadelphia. This is the second night we've pored over them. And we've decided what we're to do at Casa Grande. We're to have a telephone, as soon as the railway gets through, and a wind-mill and running water, and a new barn with a big soft-water tank at one end, and a hot-water furnace in the new house and sleeping porches and a butler's pantry and a laundry chute—and next winter in California, if we want it. And Dinky-Dunk blames himself for never having had brains enough to plant an avenue or two of poplars or Manitoba maples about Casa Grande, for now we'll have to wait a few years for foliage and shade. And he intends to have a playground for little Dinky-Dink, for he agrees with me that our boy must be strong and manly and muscular, and must not use tobacco in any form until he is twenty at least. And Dinky-Dunk has also agreed that I shall do all the punishing—if any punishing is ever necessary! His father, by the way, has just announced that he wants Babe to go to McGill and then to Oxford. But I have been insisting on Harvard, and I shall be firm about this.

That promised to bring us to a dead-lock, so we went back to our house-plans again, and Dinky-Dunk pointed out that the new living-room would be bigger than all our present shack and the annex put together. And that caused me to stare about our poor little cat-eyed cubby-hole of a wickyup and for the first time realize that our first home was to be wiped off the map. And nothing would ever be the same again, and even the prairie over which I had stared in my joy and my sorrow would always be different! A lump came in my throat. And when Olga came in and I handed Dinky-Dink to her she could see that my lashes were wet. But she couldn't understand.

So I slipped over to the piano and began to play. Very quietly I sang through Herman Lohr's Irish song that begins:

In the dead av the night, acushla,When the new big house is still ...

But before I got to the last two verses I'm afraid my voice was rather shaky.

In the dead av the year, acushla,When me wide new fields are brown,I think av a wee ould house,At the edge av an ould gray town! I think av the rush-lit faces,Where the room and loaf was small:*But the new years seem the lean years,And the ould years, best av all!*

Dinky-Dunk came and stood close beside me. "Has my Gee-Gee a big sadness in her little prairie heart?" he asked as he slipped his arms about me. But I was sniffling and couldn't answer him. And the cling of his blessed big arms about me only seemed to make everything worse. So I was bawling openly when he held up my face and helped himself to what must have been a terribly briny kiss. But I slipped away into my bedroom, for I'm not one of those apple-blossom women who can weep and still look pretty. And for two blessed hours I've been sitting here, Matilda Anne, wondering if our new life will be as happy as our old life was.... Those old days are over and gone, and the page must be turned. And on that last page I was about to write "*Tamám shud.*" But kinglike and imperative through the quietness of Casa Grande I hear the call of my beloved little *tenor robusto*— and if it is the voice of hunger it is also the voice of hope!

THE END

Milton Keynes UK
Ingram Content Group UK Ltd.
UKHW050037220624
444555UK00004B/439

9 789361 474644